The Passion Priestess

—

Temple Tales

by Stephanie C Starla

PUBLISHING HOUSE

Index

For Goddess Persephone,
your wisdom lives on...

Chapter 1

Her hands were on fire. Slowly sliding them over his back, heat rose through her body. Feeling his heart beat harder in his chest, she knew he was nearing release. The energy between them was spiralling upwards, serpent-like peaking at their crown.

The magick of life moved through every cell of her being as she closed her eyes and inhaled deeply. Calling the ecstatic vibration to her hands, they moved up the back of his heart and over the nape of his neck. His whole body shook as he let out an earth-shattering rumble from the depths of him. That was her cue to gently, lightly, stroke down his arms and step back.

It was always a beautiful sight to Cora, witnessing a man's ecstasy from her touch. Feeling his release flow through him, not just his phallus, but through his skin, eyes, mouth and hands - the essence of pure creation flowing through his being.

Cora got to experience her own too. This was what she was in service to do. Having had the call to become a Priestess of the Sacred Rites and Mysteries here, in the Temple of Persephone. She knew from a young age that her hands could evoke an energy that at first frightened her. So alive, so potent. It could bring grown men to their knees in pure ecstasy. This was her soul calling and she loved the power that ran through her. The power that helped her empower those that came to the Temple was to experience the essence of pure, sexual, creative energy.

* * *

Fear shook Cora as she learned her fate from The Oracle attending her coming of age ceremony. At only thirteen, she was to live the life of a Temple Priestess. Stories of the Temple mysteries had filled her childhood. Always intrigued by the public ceremonies and the Priestesses who held them. What happened behind the Temple doors was still shroud in mystery. Doors that warriors, Prince's, redeemed merchants, high-class women from Athens walked through and hours later, left forever changed. Childhood memories of playing with friends at the Temple steps, witnessing people come in and out, her imagination alive with what went on in there.

Only one month after her thirteenth birthday, weeping, she said farewell to her family and home. With clutched hands, her mother accompanied her to the Temple. Studying each other with swollen eyes, they embraced for the final time, both knowing life for Cora would never be the same again. Looking back to her mother, she climbed the temple stairs and walked through the door, knowing her childhood would soon be a distant memory.

In complete awe of her surroundings, she stood in the Temple hall, breathing in the intoxicating scent of lily. The cold stone and marble surrounding her made her shiver, a stark contrast from the still hot, dry air outside. Rooted to the spot she looked above, the ornate ceiling feeling so far away, the strong pillars holding it there. A glint of gold on the doors to the inner chambers caught Cora's eye. It was all she had imagined and yet nothing of what she expected.

She noticed movement from the corner of the hall and was alerted to a tall, curvaceous woman, robed in purple, silently floating towards her. Raven dark hair flowing behind, veil-like. Cora looked at her face, there was no smile on her lips, but there was warmth in her eyes. Shivering again, though not from the coolness of the stone, Cora took her all in. She had been around Priestesses before, their robes royal blue; she couldn't recall ever seeing one dressed in purple.

"Good morning Cora. I am Ophelia, the High Priestess of thi s Temple. Come with me; let's get you to the ceremonial hall where you can meet the others."

Ophelia's words were clear and concise. They had the air of authority that didn't leave you questioning but instead following.

Her pace quickened to keep up with her new mentor. Studying her back, she noticed the golden rope snaked around Ophelia's waist, the way her hair skimmed it as it trailed down her back. *Who was this woman?*

Ophelia led her to two expansive, elmwood doors. Turning the golden handle and walking through, instantly the room silenced. Peering out from behind Ophelia, Cora could see a group of young women, all her age. With them were the Priestesses she had seen in the public ceremonies. Joining them in the circle, she waited for her next instruction.

That was ten years ago now. Cora remembered when thirteen young women, all thirteen years of age, spent their first day and night as trainee Priestesses, known as the Melissae. She remembered how the excitement, fear and intrigue had filled her all at once. It seemed like another lifetime ago now and yet she could remember every detail.

It was that day she met Helia. They were placed together to share chambers though they had shared much more than that in the last ten years. Tears, laughter, secrets. Their friendship blossomed into true sisterhood. They were known as 'the twins' as they were never apart yet couldn't have been more different.

Cora with her unusual golden blonde hair, azure blue eyes and outgoing nature. Helia, her eyes an intense hazel and flowing brown hair. Where Cora's body curved, Helia's was willowy. They looked nothing alike, yet their bond was blood deep. They had taken every step of this journey together. Now, at the age of 23, they were ready to embark on a new chapter within Temple life.

Ten years of training had shown them the magick and power they held within them. To heal and explore their sexual energy and help others to awaken their own. The initiations had rocked them to their core. They had to forget everything they knew about themselves and unleash their powers. Sometimes the initiations had been gruelling – others pleasurable, yet each had taken them deeper into themselves. These years later, they felt truly at one with who they are and their soul purpose in the world. They had the power in their hands to induce pure creation and that was a responsibility bestowed onto them in dedication to their Goddess.

Cora laid in her chambers, unable to sleep. Unsure why thoughts of the past were keeping her awake. Reminiscing about her 18th Birthday initiation, the first time she was gifted a patron to serve. Her training up until that moment had been solely for herself. Journeying through her inner labyrinth of her soul. Finding her powers, her pleasures within. With her patron, she would be guiding them through theirs for the very first time. Cora could feel the flutter of nervous excitement to share her gifts wrapped up in fear she would forget her training and leave them both lost.

The memories came flooding back.

* * *

The stirrings of transformation awakened Cora as she anointed herself in a cleansing bath of rose oil. The faint scent of rose still on her skin as she moved into the ceremony chambers – silky, red fabrics draped from the ceiling with candles lighting up the stone wall. The soft animal furs warming her feet as she called in the Goddess to embody her.

The Divinity of kneeling in the chamber's centre, her heart opened to receive the Goddess's essence. Their energy entwined as it lit up her body, mind and soul.

Calling in the directions. North, East, South and West. All that is above and all that is from the Earth below. Her sex opening to receive the golden glow of pure, creative, sexual energy. Feeling it move up through her, awakening every cell of her being, spiralling upwards like a dancing serpent.

Cora remembered the very first time she called the Goddess in this way. Marvelling at how her body had tingled all over, her sex opened to receive. The pulsating in her vulva made her wet, feeling it spread to her inner folds, a thickening within her as the pulse deepened.

Mastering the act of ecstasy through surrendering to her deepest pleasures, she didn't need to stimulate physically. Flashbacks of that first time, her body shaking, back arched, head falling back. Her breath deepening as gentle moans filled the room. The everyday practise of opening to the ways of the Goddess was delicious; surrendering to be with the Goddess in this way was to alight her sexual energies within.

For the first time, she would create a sacred space to serve one of the Temple patrons. Robed in a soft, flowing white gown, Cora had spent the morning picking wild Irises. All the self and sacred space rituals were complete and after weaving a flower into her hair and placing the rest in a vase, she was finally ready to be of service. The sacred rituals that would ignite the sexual flow between her and her patron were about to begin.

Hearing footsteps coming towards the ceremonial chamber, she closed her eyes, already feeling the swirling energy between her legs. The door opened and Ophelia, her High Priestess, walked in, followed by a man. Ophelia led him to the centre of the chamber where Cora stood. Circling behind him, she laid her hands gently on his shoulders. The ceremony had now begun.

Chapter 2

All you could hear was the thumping of their hearts as Ophelia announced, "You are now in the presence of the Goddess. She will guide you through the labyrinth to your divine energy source. Do you surrender to her?"

The man, with bowed head, replied, "Yes."

Ophelia moved to the far Northern corner of the room; sitting upon a fur cushion, she nodded to Cora; this was her cue to begin.

With her heart racing, Cora could feel herself still in her mind. Surrendering to her breath, closing her eyes, she could feel his presence. It was time.

The man kneeled in front of her. His musk and longing filled the room. It didn't matter what he looked like, his history, or where he came from. Right now, her senses were alight with his sexual being, the Goddess guiding her as she connected with him. Sensing his energy coiled at the base of his spine, noticing how it began its spiral upwards only to hit a barrier around his heart and quickly recoil back down. Over and over again it played out this restrictive dance. A deep knowing inside of her moved her body to begin the rituals to release the barriers restricting his flow.

Kneeling in front of him, her left hand found the centre of his chest. That first touch lit her up. Their connection was profound as they started to become one. Lifting his blue tunic from where it pooled on the floor, she stood from kneeling, gently raising it over his head and placing it in the corner of the room.

Instantly the warmth of his body reached out to her. She noticed his dark hair curled upon his chest, his thighs, his manhood, his upper torso rising and falling in deep, heavy breaths.

Moving to the West corner of the room, she poured water into the bowl, already filled with healing oils. As soon as the water hit the oils, the fragrance of rose, lily and sandalwood circled the chambers. Her patron inhaled and she could sense him relax. The alchemy of the water and oils infused, placing a soft cloth in the bowl, squeezing it out to release the excess water, she returned to him, washing it over his face and neck. His body was receptive to her nourishing touch.

Back and forth, she moved from bowl to man. Cleansing his chest, torso, back, his sex. His phallus moving from hard and wanting - to relaxed and soft as the warm cloth and healing oils relieved him. Already she could sense the barrier near his heart begin to dissolve, his inner serpent moving upwards from his base, up through his energy centres.

Cora could sense the energy embrace the opening of his heart, his creative hands, and his mind's brilliance. Knowing it would then spiral back down again, the rhythm of serpent moving upwards and downwards creating a vibration that would soon have him releasing through phallus, throat, heart and soul. But not yet – the ceremony had only just begun.

Heating the sacred oils in her hands, she softly asked him to lay face down upon the furs. Whispering secret incantations into her glistening palms, letting the warm, activated oil drizzle down his spine, she felt him shiver, his body so receptive to her touch. Slowly moving her hands over his thirsty skin, his soft moans filling her ears as he exhaled his pleasure.

Candlelight bounced of his glistening back as the alchemy of her essence, mixed with the oils, moved into every cell of his being. Their healing nature blending through the tissue to relax him, bone-deep.

Her hands worked over his shoulders, his back, buttocks. Circling down his thighs, his tight calves and over the base of his feet. His body coming alive beneath her fingers. She knew this man had never experienced such a deep sense of peace in his body and mind.

Laying soft, dry clothes over his back to drink up any excess oil, she noticed there wasn't much. His skin was parched. Softly instructing him to turn over, she placed cloths over the length of his body and moved to the crown of his head. Gently massaging the oil through his curly, dark hair, she let the oils seep in as she pressed and circled over the tender points of his skull. His eyes flickered as she placed a slight pressure around the base. *Yes, let it all go, let it all be released.*

Splaying her hands across his chest, she noticed movement under the cloth around his sex. Her hands glistened as she moved them through his dark hairs. His breathing started to pick up, transporting him from deep relaxation to the arousal of anticipation. Moving from his crown to his right side, the side of the masculine, she allowed the Goddess to guide her. All her training over the last five years was within her. She surrendered to the wisdom of both. Removing the cloth from his body, she could see his erection. Strong and hard. The energy pulsating there, wanting, needing to be witnessed.

Feeling his muscles ripple as her hands skimmed over his torso, Cora slowed her flow. There was no rush. While he lay within her chamber, there was no time. He was Hers. He had surrendered to Her, to the Goddess. Cora knew her soul purpose was to be of service to Her also. This man had come to the Temples to be blessed. To be taken into the very depths of his being. To realise and unleash his potent, creative energy so that he could take it into the outer world, into his life work. He would achieve success. Knowing success as creating a life you love. By surrendering to the Goddess, he was surrendering to creation Herself.

These chambers were not of sordid tales. They were of pure, potent pleasure. Allowing for the release of the inner serpent to be freed from behind any barriers that were created through old, non serving programmes of the ego mind. To let it move freely through the body and sacred energy centres. This ceremony was to be led into the inner labyrinth of the sexual essence of self and once there, alchemising with it, to take it back with you to the physical world; to work with, play, create and rejoice.

Cora had been initiated in these rites over and over for the last five years. Now, in her first engagement with this physical, masculine energy, she was able to lead him to his own ecstatic flow.

Feeling the deep pulsing of his wanting, her hands moved down through the thick of hair around his fully erect phallus, the serpent circling through his sex, demanding attention. Curling her fingers around his shaft, she knew his body longed for touch. The tension was rising as his breath began to peak; she gently massaged him at his base.

Her hands moved over the crown of his penis, sensing the serpents head wanting to release. With one hand she continued to massage his sex, her other placed on his heart. This movement brought his attention from his sex upwards. His consciousness disrupted from the heat and calling of his manhood, up to his heart. A fleeting, puzzled look flashed over his face and she knew the serpent was moving from the head of his throbbing phallus to where her hands lay upon his chest.

Yes, yes, come to me, let this potent energy move into your heart, your hands, your mind.

His whole body began to pulsate - the vibration moving skywards. Cora could visibly see his body shake as the energy, once focused only on his penis now moved through every part of him. The serpent journeying towards her hands upon his heart. Rippling through waves of pleasure it danced up through his body, past her hand, into his throat. His loud groan voicing his delight as his body convulsed in pure ecstasy. Cora could tell that his logical mind was confused, her hand no longer on his phallus, which now softened, yet he continued to feel the climatic waves, usually only felt in his sex - travelling through him.

His back arched with legs stretched out, his hands gripped the furs he lay on. The feeling was intense. He felt like his head was going to explode with undiluted pleasure. His inner serpent continued its journey of spiralling up and recoiling back down, creating an inward pull of climatic energy.

Cora went to his feet and lay her palms on their base. Grounding her energy into Mother Earth, she called his climax downwards. At that moment, she sensed his sexual energy bursting through his crown. His head deepened into the furs on the ground as he let out a primal roar, his body tensing and releasing in waves.

Sensing the energy move over the surface of his being, knowing without her being there, it would dissipate, she called it down, down into her hands, through the base of his feet. This part of the ritual would ensure that his creative, sexual energy would not be lost or wasted. Instead, it would be in his physical being there with every step he took.

Cora could feel his heart rate slow a little from its climatic state. Gathering furs, she placed them on his spent body. Letting her hand linger softly on his heart, she said the words that ended the ceremony for them both.

It was only then that she noticed Ophelia, who had been there the whole time. Cora took a deep breath and let out a satisfying sigh. It was done. Her first ceremony with a patron. Her first act of service for the Goddess with another.

Ophelia rang a small, brass bell and rose to her feet. One of the younger Melissae entered the chambers to remove the used bowl of water, cloths and oils. Cora searched Ophelia's eyes for approval and she received a gentle smile and a nod. She knew she had completed her latest initiation into Priestesshood. Ophelia gestured her to follow her out of the chambers. As they went out the doors, another Melissae entered to gently awaken the man from his rest and ensure his ease in leaving the Temple.

Now she could breathe. Not realising how nervous she had been, her hands shaking as the energy moved through her. Never had she experienced such a profound moment than what she had just had. It had been a long journey for her to get here, five years of rites and rituals readying her for this moment and what a moment it had been. Something she knew she was born to do, loving how her touch could bring so much joy not only to her patron, but also to herself.

* * *

Memories of her first time kept her awake. Cora wasn't sure why; she had gone into ceremony with many patrons since that time, although her first would stay with her forever. It had changed her. She knew she was of service and what her duties were, yet it never felt like a duty. To her, it was a calling - something she loved to do and to experience.

As her reminiscing thoughts gently began to dissolve into slumber, Cora's body remembered the pulsating ecstasy of that whole experience. To give pleasure was to receive pleasure for the Sacred Priestesses of the Temple of Persephone.

Chapter 3

"Again?"

"Yes!"

"That is the third time this month!"

"I know, he said his crops have been dying."

"Hmmm. What has Ophelia said?"

"She said it's fine, which I don't understand as she is usually very strict with these things."

Pondering this turn of events, the women sat in silence. Never before had a patron visited the Temple so many times in one month. *Was it another initiation?*

"Do you think it's me? I'm not doing the ceremony correctly?" Helia asked, concerned.

"How could it be? We have been doing these ceremonies for years. I'm wondering if it's another initiation?"

"So soon? Why have we not been informed?"

"I've no idea; it could be a secret one like the one-two years ago."

Cora felt Helia tense. Yes, they both remembered that one only too well. Anxiously Helia got up from her bed and changed the subject.

"Let's go down for blessings."

There was worry in Helia's voice, yet Cora knew she would surrender them to the Goddess during their temple time. Cora had her own to share too. The weight of the last few months lay heavy on her, the sense of longing had returned and she had no idea what it was, only it left a massive hole in the centre of her being.

Hands laden with her offering bowl, the gentle hum of the Melissae filling her ears, Cora kneeled in front of the altar. Her morning walk gifted her with an abundance of marjoram and rosemary, the scent lingering on her fingers after picking them. Laying them amongst the flowers Helia had just placed there, Cora allowed herself to breathe deeply, letting all the tension from her recent heavy thoughts release on her out-breath.

Surrendering all her angst, confusion and worries to her Goddess, she moved down the altar steps and sat on the stone slabs placed uniformly, one behind the other. She pulled her white shawl further around her shoulders and joined in with the Melissae in their gentle hum.

Blessing time was to be transported into the vortex, the honeycomb centre of the Temple. The hum was to stimulate the vibration of life within them. It was comforting to Cora, allowing the frequency to awaken her, removing any stagnation - filling her. Her whole body was buzzing in harmony with her Sisters.

Helia was sitting to her left, eyes closed, completely encapsulated in the moment. Cora was pleased to see the tension held round Helia's eyes had started to soften. She hated seeing her like that. Those eyes were intense enough without the heaviness of worry adding to them.

Reaching over, she placed her hand on Helia's, sensing her deepen into her practise, all around them the harmonies of the Melissae with the Priestess calling in the Divine. The vibration of pleasure surrounding them, gifting them the sacred space to delve in, release and let go.

I'll chat with Helia later. If this is a new initiation, what could it be? Cora found it difficult to concentrate as possibilities whizzed around her mind. There had been so many. At every turn in the Sister's inner labyrinth, they would find a new adventure open up. Thanking the Goddess she had Helia with her on this journey, yet she often felt alone. Wishing someone else could take some of the quests for her, exhaustion was a surprising feeling for Cora as she contemplated another initiation. Realising her energy reserves must be low, she would have to speak to Ophelia, for she sensed there was something to uncover.

Moving through the stone corridors of the Temple, Cora instinctively knew where to head. Her subconscious taking the steps for her as her conscious mind churned over what she would say.

"Come in."

Some things never change. The butterflies had been released in Cora's stomach as she let herself into Ophelia's private chambers. Being blessed with the honour of being one of Ophelia's personal Melissae and then Priestess didn't take away from the nerves that often sprung up around her High Priestess.

"May I have some time to speak with you?"

"Yes, come, sit."

The swirling purple fabrics covering the ceiling and windows of Ophelia's room gave the illusion of opulence. However, it was no different than the one she shared with Helia, except the fabrics, that and the essence of Ophelia herself.

"What troubles you Sister?"

"To be honest, I don't know. There's something that I just can't quite see."

No sooner had the words left Cora's mouth; she knew what Ophelia's answer would be.

"Have you journeyed on it?"

"No, the truth is, I don't really want to know what it is. It feels... bigger than me."

With knowing eyes, Ophelia nodded. Having lived in the Temple for three decades, she knew the Priestess path inside and out. Her journey in and out of her own inner labyrinth brought with them wisdom. Sometimes she wished she could make the journey for her Sisters and yet knew that it was their path and purpose to do it alone.

"There is something else also." Cora tentatively shared.

"Yes my dear, there always is with you." Ophelia replied light-heartedly.

Laughing at how well Ophelia knew her, Cora relaxed and began to reveal what had been troubling her, "True – however, I'm concerned about Helia. I think she struggles with her new patron and is confused about why he has returned three times this last month. We wondered if we were entering a new initiation phase?"

The words did not surprise Ophelia, knowing how connected Cora and Helia were. It was always Cora who would ask the questions, the more inquisitive of the two.

"Always so intuitive Cora. Yes, you are both entering a new initiation phase." Ophelia knew that this news wasn't what Cora wanted to hear, yet it was what she needed.

Dread filled Cora. *Another one? Had an entire cycle passed so quickly?*

"Why so heavy Cora? You have journeyed through many initiations before." Ophelia asked, concerned.

"I don't know. Perhaps I instinctively knew that it was coming. It feels big. Bigger than what I can manage. I have felt this longing, a hole within me needing to be filled, although I have no idea with what? Sometimes it wakes me in the night, throbbing and painful. Often I fantasise about what it could be, but nothing fulfils the yearning. High Priestess... I just don't know if I can do this."

Her sobs filled the room. Fears that she once kept secret now out to be heard. All of her past came rushing back. Her mother's troubled face as she waved goodbye at the temple doors, facing the wrath of her dark Sister within her, his huge hand slapping her face, all those dark nights of the soul where she cried herself to sleep. Each painful memory came flooding back.

The warmth of the furs Ophelia had placed on her back was soothing, but the sobs kept coming. Her pain felt ancient, not just hers but all Sisters before her. Ophelia's soft incantations washed over her, the warmth of her hand on her back as she gently rocked. Cora's release had been a long time coming, where from? She didn't know.

Returning to her chambers, Helia took one look at Cora and ran over.

"What happened? Are you unwell? Oh my Cora!"

There were no more tears. Through red-rimmed eyes Cora assured Helia, she was fine.

Sighing in relief, Helia said, "I think you need to rest. Have some sleep. Then you can tell me all about it in the morning."

"Thank you. I'm not even sure I have the words. I went to speak to Ophelia about the new initiation and I just broke."

"New initiation? Is it? What will it be this time? No, let's wait until you have rested."

Gratefully Cora climbed into bed. It wasn't long before Helia could hear her deepening breaths. She knew she would never get to sleep with thoughts swirling about what this new initiation could be; Helia knew she was destined for a long night of unanswered questions.

Memories of that previous initiation two years before haunted Cora in her sleep and Helia in her thoughts.

* * *

When her new patron entered the room, Cora's senses instantly heightened. There was something about this man, guarded, hidden, dangerous even. He was unable to look into her eyes; instead they darted around the room. Trusting in the Goddess, she began the ceremony hoping that her instincts were wrong.

No sooner had she began to wash him down, something shifted. His body tensed under her touch; his muscular back rippled before he flipped over and launched into his attack.

Face stinging, Cora grappled with his weight as she tried to get from underneath him. Her muscles screaming as she kicked and punched, all of her training forgotten.

"You will not defy me, whore!" Fingers squeezing around her throat, stopped her from screaming out.

How had this happened?

A few minutes before, he was relaxed, open. His barriers dissolving. In a flash he was on top of her. His hands frantically searching under her gown, ripping at the cloth, her skin. Within seconds his full weight pinned her down, his sex jabbing at her hips, thighs, intending to take her.

The sound of his thick hand cracking against her cheek echoed in her ears. Sharp pain searing through her.

I'm going to die. This animal is going to kill me.

Fear rising again as she contemplated the end of her life.

Surely not like this. Not here in this sacred space.

An urgent whisper ran through her.

Surrender.

Legs flailing, torso contorting.

Surrender.

Laboured breathing filled the room as the fight continued.

Surrender.

Huge hands squeezing her wrists, pinning her to the floor.

Surrender.

At last, she heard the inner voice - the voice of wisdom, of the Goddess, of her training. *Yes, Surrender!*

With a mighty exhale, Cora let go. Let go of the fight; let go of the fear. Let go of the need to push back. After an initial look of surprise, urgency took over him, his fingers bruising her skin as he spread her legs and prodded the end of his penis towards her opening. Her body limp; she could no longer feel him on her. Deepening into the labyrinth, she called upon her Goddess to guide her. Reaching her hands out, she felt cool fingers lace in her own, pulling her around the corner of the inner labyrinth.

NOW!

Her thighs quickly crossed over as she flipped onto her front; from there, his enlarged phallus was locked. His scream filled the whole Temple as she jumped up to her knees, squeezing her thighs together, rolling behind her; his pain was evident. Leaping over to the Northern wall, she opened the small chest and removed the razor-sharp athame. Spinning around, she launched it from her hand. It plunged into her attacker's kidneys. The Melissae ran into the room. The shock on their face as they witnessed this deranged animal, blood pumping out of his back, rolling on the floor screaming. Cora backed up to the Northern wall; two of them ran out, raising the alarm.

Within moments Ophelia entered, wild-eyed she scanned the room. Reaching for the small dagger lodged in her golden sandals, she kicked the man onto his side, mounted him and held it over his jugular.

Seeing him as she had entered the room, the shock dissipating from his eyes, she knew he was drawing up power to attack them all. His size would mean it wouldn't be hard. The pain in his penis and kidneys fuelling his adrenalin, making it easy to kill them all in his wrath. She had seen this misplaced sexual energy before. It was why she taught all the trainee Priestesses how to become aware of it and what to do when it was unleashed.

"You dishonour the Goddess in Her Temple? You signed your fate".

Swiftly she sliced through his throat, his body going limp as a pool of blood spilt across the floor.

* * *

Hours later, with shaking hands, Cora brought the cup to her lips and let the mead's warmth soothe her aching throat. Even with blankets wrapped around her and the heat from the fire, Cora still felt chilled. Her mind numb, not knowing what to think. Fleeting moments of pain, anger, sorrow only to be followed by nothingness. Since entering the Temple at thirteen, Cora had only ever felt safe here. Never once did she think she was in danger. Now that knowing had been stolen from her and she could feel fear around every corner.

Helia, who was curled up beside her, continued to stroke her hair. Whilst her worried eyes were scanning her dearest friend. Never before had she seen Cora so vacant, her usual bright energy snuffed out. The redness in Cora's face had started to turn purple in patches; her beautiful blue eyes had disappeared into the folds of skin that now swelled around them. She looked so tiny and frail, so lost and frightened.

The image of his snarl haunted Cora each time she closed her eyes. She couldn't get the feeling of his weight from her body. Her whole body felt irritated; she could smell him on her - his breath, sex, blood. Scrubbing at her skin with her nails, she tried to remove him, to get him off her mind.

"Cora stop! You're bleeding." Helia placed her hands upon Cora's.

It was fascinating to Cora to see how red and inflamed her arm had got, the small, red spots starting to appear. No recollection of doing this to herself, of drawing her own blood.

"Let's get you to bed; drink up your mead. It will help you sleep."

While Helia took Cora to bed, Ophelia and the other Melissae removed the body and cleared the chambers of blood.

Only once before had Ophelia had to take the life of another, that time, to protect her virtue. Even with her training, it shook her. Knowing it was part of her vows to protect the Temple Priestesses, she was a life-giver, not a taker.

Facing your fear head-on was always part of the Priestess initiation. Often Ophelia knew what fear the trainee Priestess would face; this one had surprised her. Never did she think Cora's greatest fear was to be raped and killed by a man.

Knowing Cora, since the age of thirteen had been gift-ed time with the Divine Masculine within the men who were the Temple patrons, Ophelia wondered where this fear had manifested, remembering the sight of Cora, pinned to the Northern wall, eyes wide and frantic. Yes, Cora's initiation through fear had been a gruelling one for them all.

Chapter 4

Three days and nights, Cora slept fitfully. Dreams of him killing her, raping her, had her screaming out in fear. Her brow wet and sheets lay damp from the sweat of her body. Helia stayed by her side the whole time, sweeping cooling cloths over her forehead, whispering incantations to break her fever.

On the fourth day, Cora awoke to feel a little disorientated. The first person she saw when opening her eyes was Helia, smiling at her warmly.

"Morning, sleepy one."

"Morning," Cora replied roughly, her throat still dry and painful. "How long have I been asleep?"

"Three days now, you became quite unwell with a fever. It only broke last night." Helia replied concern spread across her face for her dear friend.

Cora looking down at her hands, suddenly filled with a hot flush of shame. Shame for what had happened and remorse for her Sister having to look after her. Longing to wash it all from her, she threw back the sheets and swung her legs round to the side of her bed.

"Be careful Cora!" Reaching out to steady her as she swooned, Helia sat on the bed beside her. Nausea rising as Cora's head spun, Helia grabbed a bowl seeing how pale Cora had gone. She knew she wasn't far from being sick.

* * *

It had taken Cora days before she felt strong enough to finally leave her chambers. Weeks before she returned to her Temple service. Ophelia had granted her time to join the Melissae's daily tasks instead of her Priestess ones. Secretly Cora worried that she might never be able to return to them.

Each day Cora served the other Priestesses, collecting the herbs and flowers to create the healing oils. Ensuring the jugs of water in the ceremonial chambers were warm. Cloths were clean and dry. She was enjoying collecting the berries and roots to dye the Priestesses robes. Anything that kept her hands and mind busy.

Knowing that it wasn't just her who was shook from what had happened, all the Temple Sisters were on high alert, checking in on Priestesses undertaking the sacred rites in the ceremonial chambers, listening out for any sounds of attack. It was a strange time. Never before had Cora experienced this sense of underlying fear in their day to day lives here at the Temple. Ophelia shared with Cora; that this was her initiation to face her fears - leaving her feeling guilty. Why should her fears affect the whole Temple?

Ophelia knew the reason for this; Cora was a powerful Priestess, her dedication to the Goddess, up until now, unwavering. Knowing her future path could well be that of the next High Priestess, it didn't surprise Ophelia that Cora's fears would have a ripple effect on all of the Temple and beyond.

Word had got out about what had happened behind Temple doors. When the man didn't return to his Merchant life, there were questions asked. Whispers about the Goddess taking him, eating him whole for his attack against Her. He was known to be a ruthless, abusive man. Taking what he wanted and killing anyone who got in his way.

At times Ophelia questioned the Goddess, *Why did you invite him here, to our sacred space?* Yet, truthfully she knew the answer. It was all part of moving inwards through the labyrinth of her soul, meeting and overcoming deep-seated fears along the way.

Cora's initiation and journey in this were still needing to be healed.

Ophelia asked one of her Melissae to bring Helia to her. It was time to begin the healing rites for Cora. Until now, she had left Cora to heal her way, but now she needed her to return to her Priestess service for her own sake.

It didn't take long for Helia to enter the room, always so efficient and willing to help. "Yes, High Priestess? How can I serve you?"

"Have a seat Sister. I called you here as I need to speak to you about Cora." Helia nodded; she had been waiting for this conversation and was surprised it had taken Ophelia so long to call on her. "It has been many weeks now since Cora's attack. Since then, she has been performing the tasks of the Melissae; however, it was time now she returned to her Priestess service."

"Yes High Priestess, I have to agree. Cora is missed amongst her Sister Priestesses and I know, although she is scared, she misses the rites and ceremony too."

Nodding in agreement, Ophelia shared with Helia what she would like her to do – leaving Ophelia's chambers, she quickly got to work.

* * *

Wondering why her body still ached, even though her wounds had healed, Cora was exhausted at the end of her daily duties. This exhaustion never really seemed to lift from her. She awoke from a fitful night's sleep and was met with fatigue each day. *Will it ever be the same again? Is this heaviness mine to carry for all time?*

Returning to her chambers, she was met at the door by Helia, an unexpected spark in her eyes and with urgency in her voice, she asked Cora to follow her.

Through the stone corridors, they went to the West Wing of the Temple. At the far end, they began the descent downwards, each step spiralling to the next. Cora knew they were going to the ceremonial baths, the scent of the fragrant waters drifting up to greet her on the staircase.

Cora didn't know if she had the energy to bathe one of the Priestesses and perform the cleansing rituals. She wondered why it was happening so late in the day. *They must be preparing for a patron on his travels passing through the City*, she thought.

Arriving at the ceremonial space, she was surprised to see the room empty, yet one of the baths full, candles lit and furs laid out on the floor. *Perhaps one of the Priestess are on their way?* Cora pondered.

Two Melissae came purposely towards them; only then did Cora realise that she was the Priestess to receive the ritual - backing away from them, fear rising in her chest. *I can't do this. I can't go back to my Priestess duties.*

Stopping, the puzzled Melissae looked between Helia and Cora, unsure of what to do next.

"Cora, all is well Sister." Helia soothed.

"I can't. I can't go back into service." Fear gripped Cora, her eyes wide in panic.

"Truly, all will be well. You are not going into a ritual with a patron this evening. These healing baths are for you, Sister."

From out of the shadows, they heard a voice, "Cora, your initiation period is coming to an end. It is time to begin the soul healing journey. Trust us. Surrender to Her. It's time." Ophelia emerged, anointments in hand. The fear beginning to let go of its grip around her heart, Cora could feel her body move towards them.

Yes, it was time. This soul-deep ache will heal. All I need to do is surrender. Allow.

Stepping towards Cora, the Melissae began to remove her robes. Goosebumps rose on her skin from anticipation. Many times she had experienced the cleansing ceremony, but this time it felt different. The intention to cleanse, clear, heal and restore was thick in the air. For the second time in so many months, Cora could do nothing else except completely surrender to the Goddess, her Priestesses and the Melissae. Without realising she had lost it - the trust for them all started to return.

Gently stepping into the warm water, a Melissae at each side guiding her, Cora allowed herself to entirely descend into the healing waters. Rose petals lacing over her skin, the milky waters making her body feel weightless. As the Melissae poured scented flow over her head, the tension that clung to her body started to unfurl. With every breath, her tired, aching bones relaxed more.

It felt like hours laying there, submerging deeper. Cora felt her cells open up to receive the moisture needed to flush out the toxins, which were slowly poisoning her. The gentle hum of the Melissae soothing her mind. Every so often, a rush of warm water encircling her as they poured from what seemed like endless fountains held within the jugs.

The heavy fog which had plagued her mind started to clear as her face dampened with her streams of tears. Tears of pain, of shame. Tears of hurt and betrayal. They all flowed, as did her words...

> *Winds of time come release my wild*
> *Of the ties that only I see*
> *Let me have your eyes to witness*
> *The world that shadows from me*
>
> *You whisper softly in my ear*
> *That you are not far away*
> *Yet when I turn to touch you, hold you tight*
> *Something keeps me at bay*

I see the dance of the leaves
I know they are your spirit
Yet when I try to join your dance
I somehow lose my rhythm

Winds of time come show me how
I can follow you on your flight
Lift me towards your heart
To engulf me in your light

'Sit here, be still', I hear you whisper
I feel your energy within me
I close my eyes and there you stand
In all your golden beauty

My heart rejoices with you so close
Yet I know it is just an illusion
Until I open up my eyes
To see the perfect infusion

Of white feathers dancing upon the breeze
Flowers in all their beauty
In the song of a bird, I do not recognise
All within perfect unity

And still, I rise
This I know to be true
I will always have a special place in my heart
That I know, is only, for you

It all came flooding back to her. The first time the Goddess had blessed her, entered her. After the ceremony, the words came, flowing into her sacred journal. Many years had passed since she first wrote those words and now she felt every one of them.

Cora stepped out the waters; the Melissae wrapped warm cloths around her and guided her to the furs - sitting, legs crossed, she relished her hair gently being brushed, extra furs wrapped around her body to warm and dry her.

Each Melissae was taking their time to be with Cora, giving her their full attention as they performed the rituals of adoration. Exquisite love of another. Their body, their aura, their soul. Yes, Cora knew that her soul was receiving anointments of pure love.

Feeling the golden glow of the Goddess rise within, she sensed her power grow, reclaiming what was taken from her. Calling back the power she had given him. She was returning once more.

Laying down, opening fully to receive, Cora heard the Melissae leave. Without opening her eyes, she knew that Helia was beside her. The intense energy and the natural scent of marjoram and sweet violets was the essence of her best friend and Sister.

Whispered incantations filled Cora's ears, her skin tingling as Helia's cool hand placed between her ample breasts. Breath, she hadn't realised she was holding, escaped at Helia's touch. A whole new level of opening had begun within her.

Feeling Helia slowly move to her crown, hand never leaving the centre of her chest, cradled now between her legs, Cora surrendered to her touch - feeling the energy rise from her feet to meet now two hands upon her.

Oiled hands were moving over her chest, cupping around her breasts. The intense relief of strain unlocking. The sensation of gentle pressure over her stomach, around her sides. Her Sister's soft-touch moving over her. The intoxicating spiral had begun. No longer in her head, Cora could feel her senses move down into her heart as hands massaged her body. The steely barriers were starting to lift as she let the sensations of touch, pleasure and love pour in.

For the first time in months, Cora sensed her inner serpent, the essence of her sexual energy - awaken. No longer trapped at her root, detecting its release, it began to un-coil from her womb. Gentle tingling in her sex, across her lower stomach, reaching upwards towards her heart, she felt her nipples tighten. Her Sister's hands were moving rich oils over her shoulders, down her arms, circling back up again to smooth over her breasts. Deeper, Cora fell into her pleasure.

Cora felt Helia move down to her left side, the side she knew to be of the feminine. Her now warm touch never leaving Cora, she felt their descent down her body. Those healing hands fanning over her womb. She felt a rush of emotions move through her body. As the release of pain created wells in her eyes, she let them go.

Let them all go.

Sensing Cora's deepening, Helia continued to let the Goddess guide her, knowing intuitively where to move her hands to release what no longer served. She marvelled at the receptiveness to her touch, sensing Cora's body move towards her hands, hungry for them. How blessed she felt to be able to hold this sacred space for her Sister. Knowing she would be healed from the inside out, the awakening of pleasure releasing the inner serpent from imprisonment.

Moving her hands down Cora's luscious thighs, she could feel their power, the power it would have taken to kick her attacker off her. Tears flowing from her eyes as the guilt for not being there, not protecting her beautiful Sister, rose. This ritual wasn't only for Cora; when Ophelia had asked her to create a ceremony for her, they knew it was for them both.

Like dancing embers in a fire, each one alighting the next, delicious heat skipped over Cora's body. Never before had she felt so completely alive. Helia's touch moving over her thighs, knees and down to her feet. Curled fingers around her ankles, sensing her strength come back to them. Knowing the next steps she would be taking in her life. The gentle softening of her arousal as she tuned back into her life force.

Beckoning hands to move upwards, to be held there, stroked and adored. The thoughts were travelling intuitively to Helia's hands as they, like the serpent, climbed back up over her thighs, slowly moving towards her sex. Shivers of pleasure circled through her as she felt the gentle pressure of palm on her opening. Fingers stroking her mound, the gentle rocking of her pelvis forward, to connect fully with the heat rising from sacred touch. The serpent tongue was tickling her clitoris, unveiling its protruding head.

Cora being held in this way allowed the sexual energy to stimulate her senses. Electric pulses were moving from her pleasure zones into every cell of her being. This was the Goddess way, how she had forgotten it—instead locking herself away from her pleasure, her passions and allowing what had happened to imprison her, even though she always had the key. It all rushed back. The daily pleasure practices she had ignored. The power of giving and receiving pleasure. The essence of Divine touch.

Vulva opening like a flower to the sun, she felt a heaviness enter her sex, gently penetrating through her folds. Soft moans releasing from her as the weight of the rose quartz phallus entered her. Its coolness was refreshing from the heat that was emanating from within. Each time it entered and then slowly moved outwards, she could feel her silky wetness envelop it. The rhythmic flow of crystal phallus moving in and out, touching over her inner pleasure zones, the heat of hand on her mound, thumb circling her clitoris, all motions moved together in synchronistic waves of pure ecstasy.

Cora was lost in cascading pulses of pleasure, allowing each to rise and fall over her as her breath quickened. The serpent uncoiling from her womb, spiralling upward, massaging internally and travelling up through her torso and heart. Flicking its tongue on her erect nipples while continuing its journey upwards. Passing over her throat, past her inner eye, completing the cycle of climax as it entered her crown to begin the cycle again.

Helia sensed Cora was nearing climax, her beautiful body moving snake-like upon the furs, her mouth open, small, delicious moans coming from her. The flicker of her eyes as her pelvis tilted forward and her head fell back.

Yes Sister, allow yourself the pleasure of ecstasy, enable the Goddess to bless you with your Divine right to explore your sexual, sensual being. It is so. It is so. It is so.

Cora's release was powerful, body shaking she felt it travel through her being - experiencing this massage from within, all her nerve endings receiving a blessing of power, the power of pure creation, calling it to her feet, her fingertips. She absorbed it in her heart and throat, willing it to her crown and over her glistening skin. Ecstasy was hers. To the Goddess, she would be forever grateful.

* * *

The memory of that time was engraved into her soul. The initiation of more than two years before was a powerful one. It had changed her on many levels. Cora knew that this one would do the same.

Chapter 5

Temple life went on smoothly. Even though Cora and Helia could feel that a new initiation was just around the corner, there were still duties to be carried out.

Standing in her favourite meadow, the breeze catching her hair, Cora let the fresh scent of rose and flowery anemone wash over her. This was her favourite part of the day. With the sun rising, her basket full of petals heavy with morning dew which Cora collected to give to the Melissae. It was a gift from her to help them create the ritual oils and baths, with always some leftover as a gift to her Goddess to place upon the temple altar.

Never tiring of her morning ritual, walking barefoot amongst the tall grasses and flowers, grounding into Mother Earth. Each step gifting her with a pulsation that met her heart's own rhythm. On these daily walks, she felt so in tune with the Goddess. Divinity never more than a pulse away. It was strange to her to think of not doing this every day, of what her life could have been. No doubt having a brood of children by now to nurture. If she were back in her village, it would be strange if she didn't have a husband and children yet, at the age of 23, it would have been demanded of her.

Following the calling onto the Priestesses path meant that was not her fate. Loving children as she did, spending time with them when performing in the City ceremonies. Playing with them, adoring how they dressed up as little Priestesses, robes tied around tiny necks, flowers laced in their hair. It was just she didn't have a longing for her own. Instead, she was dedicated to her soul path and to the Goddess, to be of service to Her. That was what filled Cora up.

Over the last few months, doubts had begun to seep in. *Perhaps the hole inside of her was a calling for a child?* Pondering and journaling on it, she realised it wasn't, although none the wiser to what it could be. Spending nights with Helia, speculating what the initiation would entail for them both. Helia believing that hers was something to do with the man who kept returning. On the last count, it was his fifth visit. Cora still didn't know what hers would be, although sensing it wasn't far away.

On returning to the Temple, delivering her bountiful basket to the Melissae and gifting her own scented bunch to the Goddess at her altar, Cora made her way to the ritual baths to begin the cleansing for a day with her chosen patron. Humming as she got herself ready with the assistance of her Melissae, she was a little taken aback by the butterflies dancing in her stomach. Unsure at first if it was nervousness or excitement. Deciding to settle on excitement, Cora made her way to the ceremonial chambers to greet today's patron.

Candles lit, the ritual began. Creating the space before anyone else entered was a Sacred task that raised Cora's energy. Arms stretched above, legs slightly parted, she stood in the centre of the room. Energy flowing up from the ground below. Golden light entering the soles of her feet, tingling as it stretched upwards through her calves. Feeling her sex and womb heat as the warm glow circled skywards. Heart opening to receive, with each breath filling her cells with the essence of the Goddess. The tissue in her breasts and folds of her throat softening as the energy moved upwards. Third eye-opening to the gift of insight to perform today's ritual.

A distant memory of the first patron she was blessed with flashed into her awareness. Questioning for a fleeting moment, Cora allowed her mind to empty once more as the golden glow moved up and out the top of her crown. Shivering with pleasure, she marvelled in the sensation of Her energy showering down over her pulsating skin. Never would she tire of receiving this gift. Becoming one with the essence of the Goddess was a ritual that breathed life into her very being.

Moving towards the Northern wall of the chambers and opening the wooden box, she removed the clear quartz crystals, her left hand pulsating with their weight; cupping her right hand over the top, she willed the golden essence into the stones. Programming them to hold sacred space. Placing one in each corner of the room, repeating the ancient incantations that would lift the vibrations, allowing only love, passion, pleasure and the Goddess within.

Lighting the sandalwood found in the East of the chambers, she let its smoke swirl around, clearing her aura and leaving a lingering heady scent upon the furs lying on the ground below. Walking purposefully to the South, lighting the ceremonial candle encrusted with rose petals and anointing oils. In the West, water was held in a brass bowl, dipping fingers in and splashing them over her head and face; the fragrance of rose-filled her. The final steps to the North of the chambers led her to the small statue of the Goddess, kneeling before Her Cora set her intentions. It was time to welcome her patron.

Ringing the bell to alert the Melissae she was ready, Cora took her place in the centre of the room. The power of the Goddess filling her, with closed eyes, she took in one grounding breath then opened her eyes to gaze down on her patron, curly dark hair nestled upon a bowed head.

Gently placing her hands under his chin, moving his head upwards so they could lock their gaze. Cora inhaled sharply as the eyes that met her were the eyes of that very first patron she had served all those years before.

She remembered. Secretly he hoped she would. It had been five years since she had last touched his soul. Five years of longing to be with her again. Their ritual had changed him. Never before had he felt so open, seen and adored. Remembering every moment of it, recalling her in his mind's eye, he still couldn't believe it had taken him so long to return. Every night he prayed to Persephone, her Temple Goddess, to grant him a pathway to return to her. Knowing he would have prayed directly to her if he only knew her name. Longing to say it over and over again. Wondering if it would roll around his mouth, over his tongue, the way her memory did on his heart.

Heart pounding, his eyes roamed over her body, wanting to drink her in again. Etch her in his memory for all time. It had been quite a journey to get here, kneeling before her once more. Many battles had been fought. Many women he had embraced, yet none had left him feeling the way she had. His soul longed to be with her again and being here now was a dream come true.

Knowing many men had looked at her that way, surrendering, vulnerable, lost, mixed with wanting and lust, Cora was shocked to feel the way she did now. Was it because he was her first, here in the Temple? Her own heart calling out for him to be hers. Never before had this happened. Often feeling the sexual energy between herself and her patron, Divinity's sacred connection, but this was more than that. This was an entwining of heart and soul through their gaze. Making her knees shake and her breathing shallow.

Shaking her head slightly, she returned her focus to the ceremony. Walking around his back with trembling hands, she laid them on his shoulders. Allowing her palms to connect with his energy, bringing them together as one. The rush between them rocked Cora on her feet.

This is powerful! Part of her wanted to flee from the room and the other be here with him forever. Inhaling as she bent down, she remembered his distinct musky scent. Lifting the rim of his tunic up over his back, she glimpsed the shape of him, muscular ripples she couldn't wait to glide her hands over. Feeling him shudder as his tunic was gently pulled over his head, folding it as she walked to place it in the West of the chambers and collecting the oils she had helped the Melissae make that very morning.

Missing her hands on him, he could smell the oils being warmed. Wanting her close to him so he could smell her, feel her aura entwine with his own even though he worried he would jump five feet in the air when her oiled hands eventually moved over him.

Tension building inside him, his erection full and wanting, he willed himself to breathe, relax, knowing it wasn't about taking the woman before him. What he truly desired was to be near her. The memory of her hand on his heart was more arousing than when it was clasped around his shaft. No other woman had ever been able to penetrate him in this way. Leaving him wide open to life. Remembering those weeks and months after his first blessing from her. Power rushing through him to go out and embrace life. The battles he had won, the men he had empowered to bring out the best in themselves. She hadn't only anointed his body; she had anointed his very being.

Heart skipping, Cora drizzled the warmed oils over the crown of his head, feeling it dance its way around her fingers as she ran them through his dark, curly hair. Electricity shot up through them both with each circling movement. Worrying she wouldn't be able to perform the full ritual, her legs trembling with the energy pulsing through them. It was intense. *Focus.* The mantra that Cora kept repeating over and over. Her mind springing off with questions about why she was feeling this way, what it meant, and then a lingering thought around this new initiation... *Could it be?*

Instinctively knowing where her hands would go before they reached there, already he was in ecstasy. Still not quite believing he was with her once more. Following her lead as she whispered to him to lay down on his belly, the warmth of her thighs nestled into his right side. How he wished he could sweep her up and cradle her on his knee, stroke her hair, her face. Gaze longingly into her azure blue eyes. Those eyes penetrating his very soul.

Feeling his breathing excite, Cora did all she could to slow her own heart rate. Kneeling at his side, circling over his athletic back, her hands loving the feeling of moving over his skin as if they remembered every rise and dip of his body. *Had she been so in her head when they first met that she hadn't noticed how connected she felt to him?* How she wished his large hands were exploring her body. Running over her breasts, down her stomach, fingers searching for her sex, vulva fluttering awake. *Yes! To be touched there, seen there, entered there.* Losing herself in her own secret fantasy, her hands moved down his lower back and squeezed his buttocks. Hands full of his skin, his muscle, Him.

It was becoming uncomfortable now, lying face down, erection squashed between his weight and floor below. Not daring to move, loving the feeling of her hands grabbing him, feeling the urgency of wanting more. *It wasn't just his imagination. She did want him too.* The first time they had met, he felt her commitment to him, to his pleasure. Wondering if she ever had her own. It didn't feel right to him that she wasn't receiving too. So many times he had envisioned touching her, seeing the pleasure ripple through her body, her climax held in his hands. Everything she had gifted him, he wanted to return, over and over again.

Knowing she was rushing, unable to take her time. Hands wanting to be wrapped around him, fingers running through the coarse hairs surrounding his manhood. No time for cloths to soak up the excess oils, she asked him to turn on his back. Desperate to see the unmistakable sign of his pleasure, his wanting. She wasn't disappointed.

The urgency halted as the realisation steeped in that the Goddess was no longer leading her. Taking a step back, realising this was new territory. Never before had she felt the urgency and need to touch and be touched. Consuming all of her, she searched for the Goddess within, but she wasn't there. It was just her and him, together in this space. Fear and excitement rose in tandem; with shallow breath, she froze. Not sure what to do. Feeling completely alone and unguided and yet her intuition telling her to follow her heart.

Realising she has stopped, he turned his head to see where she had gone, thinking she may be retrieving more oils. He saw her standing there, looking down at him. Fear in her eyes. *What was wrong? What had he done?* Quickly he sat up, pulling one of the furs around him. Should he embrace her or leave? Deciding to sit still, waiting for her to come out of the trance.

"Are you all right?" He gently asked her after a few minutes. Pulled back to this moment, Cora was aghast that she hadn't noticed that she had stopped the ritual.

Flapping slightly, she replied, "Yes, Yes, I am sorry. Lay back down, let's continue."

"No, let's take some time. Do you want me to call for someone?"

The thought of one of the Melissae or Priestesses knowing of what happened here brought a flush of shame up to Cora's cheeks. No, she absolutely didn't want to call for someone. Having no idea what was happening, she sat down facing him.

"I am sorry. I'm not sure what is happening here. We have met before, yes?"

She remembered! A rush of goosebumps emerged on his skin, not realising how much he had wanted her to remember. Knowing that brought a heightened sense of longing for her, one he could barely control.

Chapter 6

The energy between them was electric, filling the room with the need to find answers.

"Yes! It was five years ago now. I wasn't sure if you would remember."

"I remember. You were my first patron here in the Temple."

Her reply shocked him. *Her first?* She had seemed so confident, so powerful. Knowing exactly how to touch him, where would give him pleasure.

A comfortable silence emerged between them. Studying the other's face, drinking each other in. Tears started to fall down Cora's cheeks.

Leaning towards her, he gently wiped them away, "Do you want me to leave? Is it something I have done?" he asked cautiously.

"No. I'm just not sure what is happening. I don't even know why I am weeping? I don't want you to leave, but I am confused as to why the Goddess has left us here. Alone."

Nodding, he moved closer to her, "May I hold you?"

"Yes." The instant relief of his vast arms moving around her, enveloping her into his heart. Never before had she felt so held, so safe. To her, he felt like home.

Hoping this moment would never end, he breathed her in. Her golden strands tickling his chin, her heartbeat in unison with his own, manoeuvring himself to sitting, he gently positioned her on his thick thighs and held her into him. Wanting to keep her this way forever. Having to pinch himself to see if this was really happening or was it another dream? Feeling at peace for the first time in all these years. He was with her. She was in his arms. They were at last together.

What seemed like hours passed, just holding each other, no need for words. Being together, gently stroking, rocking. Neither knew how much pleasure could be had by being with the one you desired.

Cora was aware that the Melissae would be wondering why she hadn't rung the bell to end the ceremony and call them in. Feeling her shift out of their embrace, he knew that their time together was coming to an end. Breaking their silence, he had to find a way to see her again.

"May I ask, what is your name?"

Cora was unsure whether or not she should share it. During the ceremony, their answer would always be, *'I am the Goddess, I am the essence of Persephone.'* Never before had she thought of answering any differently. Her own name being the sacred one, only for herself and her loved ones. Taken aback by the want to share her name with him, to hear it uttered by his luscious mouth, she let it slip out.

"Cora"

"Cora" She trembled as she heard her name being said like it was an exotic word from far off lands. How she longed to hear him say it, over and over again.

"And yours?" Knowing she shouldn't ask, for the men that came to the Temple were always named Patron. Their identity didn't matter; in the ceremony, they were the patrons of the Goddess.

"Alexeii" Why did his name sound so familiar to her? Knowing she hadn't been told it on their first encounter, it felt like she had known it for a lifetime.

"Alexeii" His turn now to go weak at the knees. How he had imagined her lips making the shape of his name, to hear her voice utter the word that his soul longed for.

This was new territory for Cora. It wasn't enough for her to only know his name now. Needing to know everything about him. Where he lived. What he did all day. Did he already have a lover? Wanting to see his soul, understand Alexeii, never tiring of repeating his name.

"Can I see you again Cora?" That word again, dripping off his tongue. Feeling honoured, she had shared it with him - the anticipation of her answer holding his heart, vice-like.

"I don't know how we can? It is up to the Goddess to give you access to the Temple." Cora searched her mind for ways it could happen, knowing it wasn't within her power to grant such things. Even if he was chosen to be a Temple patron again, there was no knowing how long it would be or if Cora would be the Priestess he was granted.

"There must be a way? I know I am pushing way beyond what I know are your sacred ways Cora, but I can't leave here knowing I will never see you again."

Her heart flipped. She felt the same too. Hearing footsteps approach their chambers, she knew that the Melissae were on their way to check if their ritual had ended.

Quietly Cora whispered, "Meet me at dawn in the meadow beyond the forest, behind the temple." Springing back from him, she rang the bell to alert the Melissae to enter to complete the ceremony and prepare her patron, Alexeii, for his departure.

"You've been some time. Is everything all right?" Helia looked up from spinning wool quizzically.

"Everything is wonderful!" There was something in Cora's voice and the way she was glowing that caught Helia's attention.

Feeling Helia read her quickly, Cora busied herself with getting ready for the evening ceremonies in worship to the Moon aspect of the Goddess. She was full tonight in Virgo, which called for all Priestesses to carry out the ceremony. Feeling relieved to have something to take her mind off meeting Alexeii, there was no way Cora would have been able to sleep; a night-long ceremony was perfect. It also meant most of the Temple would be sleeping at dawn and she could leave unnoticed.

* * *

Dressed in their lunar ceremony robes of black, the Priestesses circled around their High Priestess as she called in the directions. The Melissae created an outer circle holding space for the ceremony with their distinctive hum. At first, it was gentle, an undertone that brought comfort and grounding. As Ophelia finished the opening of the ceremony, their sacred sound started to increase. Each of the Priestesses called in the essence of Lady Luna herself in their secret incantations, adding to the volume.

Heat began to rise in Cora and the others. Weaving around their feet, winding up calves as the energy rose with the sound of their voices in unison. Slowly it moved upwards, opening all of their energy centres. As their sacred sound got louder, it created a crescendo of energy bursting through their crowns. At that moment, Ophelia let out a wolf-like cry, followed by their powerful incantation to the Moon Goddess.

As is their ways on a full moon, each of the ritual Priestesses de-robed to reveal themselves skyclad. Arms raised above their heads, they called in the essence of their Lady Luna to bless them. Reaching out to link arms, each swayed and moaned in time with the hum and incantations of the outer circle of women, letting the energy of the moon move through them.

As the energy began to descend and be grounded into the earth below, they all cloaked themselves once more. Together they left the Temple and spilt out to the grounds at the rear to soak up the moonlight. Heading towards the stone labyrinth, each would take the sacred journey in and out. An intention fuelled their feet towards Her centre; once there, they would look skywards and release the thing that no longer served them to their Moon Goddess, either through words, song or howl.

Journeying back out of the labyrinth would gift them insight that would light their way to their inner power. Perhaps a new gift like heightened intuition or clairvoyance. It could be a beautiful lesson from a patron or even a new song that plays through their dream time into their consciousness. All they had to do was be open to receive.

After the final Melissae had taken their turn to walk in and out of the labyrinth, the Sisters would return to the Temple halls to celebrate with mead, moon cakes, bread, grapes, dates and goats cheese. An offering plate would be left in the labyrinth centre for the Goddess, in thanks for gifting them with soul illumination.

Cora and Helia returned to their chambers, full in body, heart and soul. Helia's eyes were heavy and ready to sleep most of the day away, knowing that sunrise was just around the corner. Cora felt more alive than ever, the anticipation of seeing Alexeii again sending tiny shock waves through her body. To Helia, she feigned sleep. Putting on her night tunic and getting into her bed-chamber, it wasn't long before she heard Helia's breath deepen and she knew she was asleep.

Waiting a while to ensure she didn't waken her Sister, Cora's mind was churning. Thoughts of her impending meeting with Alexeii. She couldn't wait to see him again, touch him, feel his arms encircle hers. Also worries that he wouldn't be there. That she would wait hours and he would not appear; his mind changed or realise that he had made a mistake. One way or another, she had to know.

Quietly Cora slipped out of bed; grabbing her day gown, blue robe and sandals, she quickly removed her night tunic and left the room naked. Closing their chamber door as silently as she could, she got dressed and took flight down the corridor towards the Temple exit.

Heart racing, she ran through the forest that protected the boundaries of the Temple and headed to her favourite meadow. Hoping that Alexeii would be there, open-armed to greet her.

Stepping into the high grasses and long-stemmed flowers, she saw him. Standing at the edge of the meadow, under a cypress tree, he stepped out onto the meadow floor. Heart-stopping for a beat, Cora felt a million butterflies take flight in her belly.

He was here!

Not quite believing it, Alexeii had to pinch himself to ensure this sight of pure beauty wasn't an illusion. Wondering whether he was still dreaming, having spent the night under the Cypress tree, unable to be too far away from her. The sight of her! Golden hair shining in the light of dawn. Cheeks pinked. *Had she ran to him?* Cloaked in royal blue, which made her eyes illuminate all the more.

The space between them at that point was too far. Eyes locked together, they finally fell into each other. Massive arms encircled Cora as she lay her cheek upon his chest, hearing the thudding of his heart, her arms snaking around his waist. Heart filling with the sensation of being home. How she could stay in these arms for lifetimes. Not knowing how she coped before without them.

Lifting Cora's chin upwards, gazing into her eyes, he felt himself drink her in. Lowering his lips, he found hers. Gentle touch at first that quickly became more urgent. Tongue seeking tongue. Hands roaming each other's back. Lost in the lust of one and other. They knelt amongst the long grasses; hidden from view, they descended further, the soft ground becoming their nest as they discovered each other's mouth, tongue, touch.

Raking fingers upwards through her thick, golden locks, Alexeii cradled her head in his hands. Tongue dancing in her mouth, luscious lips moving over his. Drinking in their lust, he couldn't get enough. Finally building his strength, he pulled his head away. Needing to know where this was going.

"Beautiful Cora, how I want to lie with you. Be with you. Hold and caress you. I want to see your milky skin, touch and feel it. All these years I have dreamt of becoming one with you. Bringing you pleasure, as you have gifted me. I know if we continue, I will lose myself in you. I don't want to dishonour you in any way." His eyes were intense, a tinge of worry in their corners. Cora didn't know whether to laugh or cry. *Yes, she wanted to be ravished by him. Made love to over and over. He was a man of honour.*

"I know our connection is a gift from the Goddess. I want you Alexeii..."

Without hesitation, his lips found hers once more. Hands gathering the hem of her day gown, gently lifting it up over her head. Pupils enlarging as his eyes devoured her. Moving back a little, resting on his elbow, he studied her body, the milkiness of her skin. Ample breasts laying upon her chest, nipples erect, waiting to be caressed - the softness of her round stomach. Gazing down to her sex, noticing how it was covered in soft golden hair. Longing to stroke and kiss her there. Voluptuous thighs leading to shapely calves, slim ankles and cute toes. She was indeed a Goddess.

She felt Divine as he made love to her with his eyes. She wasn't sure how long she could lie here without his touch. The need for him rising, a dampening in her sex calling him there. Nipples tightening like rosebuds awaiting his caress. Her own hands burning up, wanting to touch him. To be the gift of pleasure.

Tunic now discarded, he lay there naked. Remembering his body from their time in the Temple, it took on a new essence here. Outwith the ceremonial chambers, laying within the heart of Mother Nature, the sacred union of man and woman. No longer in service to the Goddess but in service to each other.

The morning light highlighted his dark stubble, chocolate brown eyes dancing with the flowers surrounding them. Raven black hair curled upon his head. Memories of her hands moving oils through it, how it had glistened. Taking in his muscular chest and torso, a thin line of dark hair leading to an expanse of more dark curls, which encircled his enlarged phallus. Thick, mighty thighs, thighs that she couldn't wait to run her hands over, yes, this man was indeed a warrior.

Chapter 7

Cupping his hands over her breast, thumb circling her tightened nipple, Cora closed her eyes and enjoyed his touch. Ten years of Temple life had gifted her with deepening degrees of pleasure. Pleasure at the Goddess's hands, herself, some patron's, or her Temple sisters during ceremony. The difference was the feeling of Alexeii's touch - the man her heart and soul desired. It was so very different from past experiences.

Astonished at how her body searched for his touch. Her back arching to have more of him caressing her wanting breasts. Pelvis tilting forward to beckon him downwards. The excitement in her womb space as his hands descended over it. Opening her legs to welcome his fingers, she trembled in anticipation of his touch. His palm massaging her golden mound, fingers circling inwards over the opening to her sex. Feeling her nectar escape from her inner folds as he dipped in, his fingertips laced with her honey. Silken touch skimming over her clitoris, sending gentle waves of pleasure through her body. Never before had she wanted to be entirely at one with a man.

Pulling his head down to her, she kissed him urgently. His gentle moans enthralled her as she moved her hands over his chest. Feeling his hard sex against her, she wanted it to be where his fingers were. Stroking down his torso, lacing her fingers around his erect phallus, she felt it pulsate. Manoeuvring herself underneath him, she caught his questioning eyes. She knew he was asking her if it was truly what she wanted.

Smiling with her eyes and gently nodding, she slowly felt her now wet vulva filling with him. The tip of him entered first, Cora marvelled at how well it filled her. Gently he pushed inwards, internally massaging her folds, she felt herself opening to embrace him. His eyes now closed, head tilted back, she saw the shadow of stubble on his neck, arching her back so she could reach up and lick his throat, he pushed in further. Never before had she felt so full. So connected. Their union complete; they were as one, locked in each other.

Better than he had ever imagined, being inside of Cora, his Goddess, was Divine. Her warmth encapsulating his penis inside of her, loving how willing her sex received him. How he had flowed into her, rocking now backwards and forwards, he could feel her pleasure release over the head of his phallus. Her eyes closed, mouth slightly open, looking down at her and wanting to take her into a delicious, climatic state.

Bodies as one, hips moving in rhythm, their lovemaking sending ripples of sexual energy into the fields surrounding them. The heat of their bodies building in pleasure and passion, nearing climax as they lost themselves entirely in the other.

Yes, the Goddess had brought these two together. As she witnessed their union, a smile spreading upon her face knowing that this initiation of the lust and love between man and woman would wake the world up more than either of them would ever know.

Laying in each other's arms spent, waves of satisfied desire moving through them, reality started to creep in. Their time together would be coming to an end. Neither wanted to utter the words that would penetrate their harmonious bubble.

"Cora, I know you have to go now. I don't want to cause you any trouble." Sighing, Cora nodded. She knew the Temple Sisters would be rising and if she didn't return hastily, she would be missed.

"I don't want to leave you, Alexeii. I could happily stay in your arms all day." Smiling, he pulled her in closer. Not wanting her to return either.

"Where are you staying? I could go for a walk after my Temple duties, around dusk?"

"In the next village. Yes, let's meet again, but we shall meet here. Will it be safe to do so?" Nodding, Cora worked out how many hours before they could see each other again. Reaching for her day gown and robe, she dressed.

"I'll need to gather some flowers and herbs for the Melissae, so questions aren't asked."

Alexeii didn't know all that happened in the Temple, but he knew of some of the Priestess duties. He had spoken to many patrons who had shared their journey and experiences. His admiration for Cora's commitment to her Temple Goddess and her service to Her, grew.

Some men wanted to own their Priestess, captivated in their lust for them, demanding they leave the Temple and stop working with patrons. He never understood that; perhaps it was his dedication as a warrior and his mission that his Being recognised the sacred ways of old. He was not entirely sure why he felt this way but instinctively knowing that what they had was special. It was between him and her, not him and the Goddess. That knowing illuminated his heart.

Leaving lingering kisses upon his lips, Cora dragged herself away. Saying her farewell's and looking forward to meeting him under the Cypress tree at dusk, she rushed back to the Temple.

Cora felt glad that she didn't have any patron duties today. The day after a night-long ceremony was a day of rest and rejuvenation. Time spent sleeping, reading and writing. Some of the Sisters spun wool or bathed one another. Also spending time by their Goddess altar in prayer and worship.

The young Melissae could be found adorning each other's hair with flowers and making circlets with them to place upon their crowns. Their faint laughter heard throughout the Temple walls.

Amazed that she didn't feel sleepy, Cora went to the kitchens to gather some bread and cheese before heading to sit near the labyrinth behind the Temple. Here she could let the heat of the sun warm her face while relieving her ravenous hunger. Each bite of bread with goats cheese alighting her senses, remembering his tongue in her mouth, searching, filling. Losing herself in the memory of their morning together, she didn't hear Helia approach.

"Where have you been all morning?" It was usually Helia that would awaken first, waking to find Cora's bed-chamber empty, she was curious as to where she had disappeared to.

"I woke early, so I went to the meadow to pick some flowers and herbs" Thank goodness she had done that too! Knowing she could not lie to her dearest friend. It was hard for her not to share this experience, but she knew deep down that Helia would never understand. She wasn't sure if she did herself.

Their conversation was interrupted when three of the Melissae ran over to them to show off their new flowery creations. Adorning both Priestesses with circlets and bracelets that they had spent the morning making, excited chatter filling the air about their experience of the full moon ceremony the night before and what their wishes and intentions had been. Cora was dragged to her feet to follow them into the forest to look for the fae folk they thought they had spotted, Helia joining them in their search.

Both women remembered their time as young Melissae. The mix of missing their family while discovering their new one. The magick that every day presented as they moved deeper into the Temple rites and ceremonies. It was a time of joy and adventure, secrets and rites of passage.

Each of the Melissae had been assigned to a Priestess to guide them through the journey. The young Phoebe was Cora's ward. She was so full of light that she was a joy to teach and care for - a little sister with a huge heart. Always the one to lead the others on adventures and a true believer in the unseen. From the faeries to unicorns, she had the magick healing touch. She was often called upon to help with a dying plant or to blend a potent healing balm. Phoebe was a true gift to the Temple and Cora knew she would be a spectacular Priestess when she came of age.

Cora filled her day napping in the shade of the forest trees, writing poetry in her sacred journal and fantasising about her time with Alexeii when the sun went down. Not sure what she would say to Helia to get away on her own, most nights after the moon was fullest, they would walk in her light together.

No matter what, it had to happen. The need to see Alexeii again, to be with him, was all she could think about. Hating to lie to Helia, yet knowing she had no choice. Praying that her Sister would not see through her untruths and catch her out.

Eating their evening meal together, Cora shared with Helia that she would walk on her own that evening. Sharing her intention to speak to Lady Luna privately about something that was bothering her, Helia's ears pricked up.

"Are you struggling with something? Can I help?"

"No, it's nothing, I'm just wondering about our new initiation and what that will look like for me. I was going to ask for wisdom from our Moon Goddess while she is in her illuminating phase," Cora replied.

"Ahh, are you sure you don't want me to come with you?"

"No, thank you. I think I need to be alone to hear Luna's message. I'm just going to get ready now". Hoping that Helia believed her, Cora left the table to get ready to meet Alexeii. Her heart was thumping as she tried not to run to her chambers to get her robe. Knowing that her haste would arouse suspicion, not just in Helia but also in Ophelia, whom she caught giving her sideways glances a few times that day.

How she wished so many astute and intuitive women didn't surround her. Knowing that she didn't want to be found out, wanting to keep what was happening between her and Alexeii to herself.

* * *

Sitting under the Cypress tree, with closed eyes, Alexeii took in the magick of the moon. Having always been intrigued with Her since being a child. Her cycles of full to dark fascinated him, knowing that her teachings were the essence of women.

The memories of his mother and the other village women, retreating to their red tent each dark moon, noticing how light they returned after three days and nights of their own private temple time. As a young man, he was not permitted into the tent, his ritual time spent once a year with the menfolk, sleeping under the moon for one entire cycle. The relationship between the Sun and Moon, the masculine and feminine, ran deep into his Being.

Watching him lay under the moonlight, his eyes closed, breathing relaxed, Cora didn't want to disturb him. *What was he thinking? Was he dreaming?* The moon illuminated his features, giving them an ethereal glow, looking like a God who had come down from Mount Olympus to be with her.

Sensing he was being watched, Alexeii opened his eyes. He was surprised to see Cora looking down at him, wondering how he hadn't heard her approach. Those sparkling eyes drinking him in, the light of the moon dancing upon her crown, his Goddess, come to greet him.

Without words, he rose; cupping her face in his hands, he leaned forward and kissed her sensually. Soft, lingering kisses passed between them. Fingertips tracing the outline of his spine as they moved up and down. Delicate breaths, not daring to break this moment of dreamy passion. Tongue's tickling the inside of their mouths, the magick linking their hearts and souls as one. The love spell cast as they lost themselves in each other.

Feeling their intensity rise, their need for intimacy increasing, hands becoming more urgent, his hand found her breast under her cloak. Softly tracing around her curve, his fingers discovered her protruding nipple, between thumb and forefinger, he gently squeezed. Pulses of desire ran straight to her sex, feeling moisture dampening her cloths, arousal thickening her inner folds, wanting him to explore more of her with those curious fingers. Her own hands moving downwards to feel him.

"No, tonight is for you, my Goddess. Your pleasures to receive", gently he manoeuvred her hands away from his arousal and laid her down on the soft ground, made from the downy branches of the Cypress tree.

Knowing the art of receiving was just as powerful as the essence of giving, Cora surrendered to his touch. Pulling the ties of her robe free, he lifted her day gown to reveal her ample, naked body. It was astounding to see how much it glistened in the moon's light, a transcendence of milky whites and opals. It was a rarity to see skin so light, hair so golden, how her skin must redden in the heat of the sun, but now, it shone in the moonlight.

Laying light kisses between her breasts and down her stomach, Cora relished in the sensation of rough and smooth. His stubble brushing her skin while his lips tenderly soothed her. The anticipation of where they would land next was nearly too much for her to bear. Large hands massaging her breasts, his tongue found the tip of her budding nipples; circling round, she gasped as a rush of pleasure ran through her, pleasure penetrating her at her very core.

Smiling at her reaction to his lightest of touches, Alexeii traced his tongue down her rounded stomach, hands still on her bountiful breasts. He moved into the mound of soft, golden curls that led towards her sacred sex. Kissing her there, seeing her pleasure glisten on her inner lips, he moved his hands down from her breasts to her hips. Moving to lay between her thighs, fascinated by how she began to instinctively open for him. Continuing his kisses over her opening, his tongue found her aroused clitoris and gently pulsated on it. Ripples of intoxicating pleasure moved through Cora. Hips pushing into his hands for more, Alexeii kept the gentle rhythm of soft pressure upon her pleasure point. Feeling her juices flow from her sacred opening, he placed his fingers inside of her, holding them there as he continued to tease her with his tongue.

The heat of her arousal rushed up to her cheeks. With the weight of Alexeii's fingers in her opening, softly filling her, the sensation of his tongue, only just touching her clitoris, she longed for more of him. Pulling his head closer to her, fingers curled around his hair as his tongue swept upwards over her clitoris. His mouth now covering her vulva, tongue circling all of her, fingers going deeper, pleasure rising higher, the intensity taking over, the power of their lovemaking peaking as she called out his name.

Hearing her howl his name to the moon was more than Alexeii could bare. Feeling her pleasure grip his fingers, moving them over her inner pleasure spot, his arousal wanting and needing to be inside of her. Not having to wait long before she called him to become one with her. Lifting his tunic to place the tip of his phallus into the opening of her, feeling her warmth call to him, her ecstasy coat him in its silky dew, hips moving forward drawing him towards her, he entered her fully. Feeling her soft folds encircling his arousal, pulling him deeper into her. Divinity was his.

Their bodies rocked together, their unity sealed in lust, passion and love. Moving in unison until both reached their ecstatic release. The wild of their bodies calling out in the night of their undenied pleasure. Waves of ecstasy began to dim into fulfilling ripples of pure bliss. Lost in each other, they lay, drinking in the moments of being together in this way.

Knowing the time was nearly upon them for Cora to return to the Temple, they started to dress. The words they knew needed to be said, lost in the silence. Walking hand in hand together, the full moon illuminating their path, they parted ways at the edge of the forest. Where once there was only pleasure, dread started to fill Cora's heart at the thought of being away from him. Turning to look up into his chocolate brown eyes, she couldn't bear to say goodbye; instead, she whispered.

"Tomorrow at dawn?"

"Tomorrow at dawn." He replied, leaning down to place a lingering kiss on her forehead. Sensing the tears beginning to spring in her eyes, she turned from him - a part of him ripping away as he watched her leave. Tomorrow couldn't come quickly enough.

Dawn and dusk were theirs, time spent talking, love-making, and getting to know each other's lives. Days went by in a blur of service and duties to the Goddess. Thoughts always on the time she had just spent with Alexeii or fanta-sising about the next. Warm nights spent lost in his arms, early mornings rushing to their spot under the Cypress tree. There wasn't much time for sleep, yet Cora had never felt more energised and alive.

Knowing that Helia and her High Priestess were aware of a shift in her, she kept her distance. Busying herself with day to day tasks. Feigning the need for time alone to process what this new initiation could be, she knew she was lying to some of the most important people in her life, keeping secrets from them in fear of what they might say, what they might do.

Each day her love for Alexeii grew. She knew now what her initiation was. She was getting initiated in matters of the heart, in pure love and devotion. One she had only previously known for her Goddess. Knowing there was room in her heart for both but scared her dearest Sisters wouldn't understand. The Goddess, her Persephone, had gifted Alexeii to her and she wasn't ready to share their love with anyone.

Cora knew outside love was deemed as forbidden for Priestesses who wanted to stay within the Temple walls. There had been Priestesses who had left the Temple for love. Moved into a neighbouring village or travelled with the object of their affection to create a home. Some had even visited with babe in arms, so grateful for their time in service to the Goddess. Remembering how happy she was for them but confused at their want to ever leave their sacred practice.

Even now, Cora had no intention of ever leaving. The thought of not being part of Temple life wrapped her heart in fear. Not knowing what the future held but sensing massive shifts on the horizon, she wasn't sure how it could all work out. Every morning after her time with Alexeii, she gave an offering to the altar, sharing her thanks to Persephone. Surrendering her fears and worries, entrusting them to the Goddess to help her see the path that would ensure her heart was whole. Her dream that she could continue to be of service as a Priestess of Persephone and be with her one true love, Alexeii.

The 'how' would all work out, she hoped.

Chapter 8

"High Priestess, I am worried. Cora feels so distant, spending so much time on her own. I know something has changed in her, yet she won't confide in me. I'm not sure what I should do?"

Helia had put off sharing her concerns with Ophelia, hoping that Cora would open up and share with her what was happening. Weeks had passed and still, Cora felt distant. Every evening choosing to be by herself, in the morning, when Helia woke, Cora's bed-chamber was empty.

It wasn't even that she was physically distant; Helia felt the emotional distance between them too. Cora had locked her out and it created unease between them. Never in all the years they had known each other had she felt that disconnected from her.

At first, she thought it may be to do with their current initiation. Helia knew that this was a transformational one. Her recurring patron sharing his feelings with her on his last visit had shocked Helia. Having experienced the lust from a patron before, she sensed his longing and love for her this time. Knowing he had mixed up his feelings for the Goddess with her, Helia had to build firm boundaries to ensure he knew that it was not her who gave him pleasure, released his creative, sexual energy. It was She, their Goddess and any feelings of love and worship were to be placed towards Her.

Praying on it during blessing times, surrendering it to her Goddess while secretly asking *why the Goddess kept bringing him to her, over and over? It felt like torture to him - and her.* Each visit, she would have to reject his advances, his proclamation of love and devotion. His want to whisk her away, asking her to be his wife. His infatuation was potent, although Helia believed, wholly misplaced. Still, the Goddess brought them together, sometimes two or three times a week. *Why?*

How she wished to share her experiences and worries with Cora. Something they often did in the evening before sleep. Now Helia returned each night to an empty room, left to ponder her thoughts on her own. *What was happening between them? Where was she going? Why was she spending all this time alone?* Several times Helia thought about following her, just to make sure she was safe. However, she never did, deep down knowing she must trust her Sister and in time, she would share with her.

"You must give her space Helia. All initiations take the journey in and out of the labyrinth and it must be done alone. You have your own to travel, do you not?" Ophelia cut into Helia's thoughts.

"Yes High Priestess, I do. I have to confess I am struggling with this one. I am unsure why the Goddess keeps bringing him to me. It feels so hard on him. Each time I say no, I can feel his heart break."

Tears welled up in Helia's eyes as she remembered yesterday's encounter. How he had begged to know her real name, something to take away with him after she had said no to his proposal of marriage. Knowing she would give her name to no man, or woman for that matter, who wasn't part of her Temple life. Her real name was sacred to her soul, only to be shared with those she could trust with her life.

"You will find your way Helia. Our Goddess has great plans for you, and you know as well as I, the only way out of this initiation, is through." Reaching out to place Helia's hands in hers, Ophelia offered some comfort and guidance. Remembering her own initiation at this stage too. How it had pulled her heart in two, something she still has to work on to heal.

"Thank you. I really just want my Sister back. I know I take this journey alone, yet it was a wonderful comfort to have her there to talk things through. I miss her."

"I know you do." Wrapping her arm around Helia, she brought her into her chest. Not wanting to share her own concerns about Cora, for she had noticed how absent she had been of late. Yes, she was always there for her service and Temple duties, but her usual full attention was not. Wondering where she was going and who with, filled her thoughts. *Will she experience her heart being pulled in two directions also?*

Although she had trust in the Goddess, she knew something was shifting within Cora and she worried that it may pull her in a direction that may leave them all hurt.

* * *

Rushing back from another memorable morning spent with her love, Cora knew it was going to be a long day before she saw him again at nightfall. Not having a patron today meant spending more time with her Sisters and that worried her. Keeping her distance from Helia had been the most challenging thing she had ever done. Longing to share her love for Alexeii with her but knowing she couldn't. Especially with Helia facing her own initiation with her patron.

Secretly she hoped that Helia would fall in love with her patron too, so they could share the journey together. That way, she wouldn't have to hide her feelings or lie to her best friend every day. Although, Cora knew how strongly Helia felt about these matters. When they had discussed falling in love with patron's before, Helia bordered on disgust at the prospect. Her devotion to love was only for the Goddess. The idea of sharing that with a man was out of the question.

Knowing that Helia would never understand kept the secret with her and only her. That was why she had to keep her distance not only from Helia but Ophelia and her Melissae, the young Phoebe too. Their intuition was powerful and their inquisitive nature would demand the truth of her. It was easy to keep from them when she was busy with her Priestess duties, but today, when there were no patron's or ceremonies to perform, she would struggle to stay away.

Like she was reading her mind, Helia appeared from the back of the Temple and walked towards her. Heart beating, wanting to turn on her heels and run back into the forest, Cora could do nothing but continue on her path, knowing Helia had seen her.

"Morning! Did you enjoy your walk?" Helia called, eyeing Cora as she began reading her body language with intent.

"Yes, yes! It was lovely. I picked some flowers, I'm just away to give them as an offering to the Goddess". Holding out the bunch of wilted flowers, she had hastily picked on her return to the Temple.

"Before you go, can we talk?" *Those eyes, boring into me. Oh Goddess, she knows!*

"Of course. Give me a minute and I'll meet you back out here. I'm parched, as are these flowers." Replying with a light giggle hoping it disguised the unease in her voice.

Watching Cora practically run towards the door to the Temple, Helia worried that her thoughts were correct. Cora was definitely hiding something from her. *But what?* Never before had this level of secrecy been between them, always each other's confidant spending endless nights sharing their worries, pleasures and fantasies.

What was going on with her? Where was she going and why was she always busying herself? Knowing she had to find out, Helia decided to follow Cora into the Temple, there were no duties or ceremonies today. It was the perfect opportunity to have a long conversation and get some answers to all her questions.

* * *

"Cora, may I speak with you?" *There really was no-where to hide!* Helia in the Temple grounds, now Ophelia in the kitchens.

"Yes High Priestess. I'm just getting some water then will be going to the altar to be with the Goddess". Hoping that would give her the permission she needed to leave the conversation, Cora looked beyond Ophelia to the drinking fountain, busying herself as if she had some urgent business to attend to.

"Get your water and come to my chambers before you go to the altar. There will be plenty of time for that later." There was no arguing with Ophelia, surrendering to the re-alisation that she was about to be probed and questioned, Cora nodded.

With a small marble vase in hand filled with meadow flowers, Cora knocked on Ophelia's door.

"Come in Cora". *How did she always know it was her?* Wondering if there was a hole in the door that allowed her to see who stood behind it, Cora stepped into her High Priestess' sacred chambers.

"Have a seat. I've wanted to speak to you for some time; however, you always seem to be busy".

"Yes High Priestess, I have been dedicated to my du-ties and practices. Also spending time in reflection." Hoping Ophelia wouldn't see the rush of red that had blushed her cheeks, Cora evaded Ophelia's searching eyes by star-ing at the flowers in her hands.

"Is that because of the initiation? Has it shown itself to you?" It sounded like Ophelia was asking Cora; however, they both knew that the answer was yes.

"Yes, I think so. I'm just letting it settle in. Focusing on my practices, taking myself away to journal and be with nature." Still avoiding Ophelia's gaze, Cora knew she was in dangerous territory. If Ophelia continued her questioning, she would see her hiding something if she didn't already.

"You know I am here for you Cora, that if you are struggling in any way, I am happy to support you, listen and perhaps even help guide you." Feeling guilty for hiding her truth from Ophelia, Cora struggled for the words that would get her out of these chambers without brushing off her help.

"I know and I am so grateful for all you do. I just need to do this one alone. I feel it is important for my inner growth." Hoping to stop Ophelia for now, Cora looked up from the flowers and connected with Ophelia's eyes. Probing eyes, reading every inch of her. Feeling Ophelia search into her soul for answers, Cora quickly stood up.

"I really should get these flowers to the Goddess. She has helped me so much recently and I want to share my gratitude."

Ophelia said no more and nodded, granting Cora the opportunity to speak her thanks as she swiftly left the room. Feeling relieved that she had gotten away without having to divulge what was really going on for her, she skipped towards the altars. Today she had many things to be grateful to the Goddess for.

Managing to avoid Helia for most of the day as she spent time with her Melissae, Phoebe. Feeling relieved that all Phoebe wanted to talk about was becoming a Priestess. So many questions about patron's and Cora's own coming of age ceremony. Phoebe's was still a few years away, having only recently had her Merarche ritual to celebrate her first bleed arrival. A beautiful day filled with shared wisdom, ceremony, and release from her child phase as she stepped foot into womanhood.

How she had cried that day, watching Phoebe leave her footprints in the sand as she placed candles in them to light her way. The poetry she had shared with her Temple sisters. Remembering Phoebe's sweet song in thanks to her elders.

Not all Melissae experience their first bleed within the Temple, some having started before they arrived at the age of thirteen. Most would have had some form of ceremony to celebrate and if they hadn't, they were welcomed to have their own held by their Sisters. Cora, having her first bleed at eleven, had hers at home. Her mother, aunt's and grandmother's around her. Sharing their experiences of womanhood, their stories of their own coming of age. Remembering the little gifts she had received. A small jar of scented oils, a tiny marble statue of their Goddess Persephone, little did she know at eleven that she would be one of the Temple Priestesses. It was a beautiful ceremony for her. It was a sacred time that she enjoyed creating space for the other Melissae.

Chapter 9

Cora was in high spirits when she sat down with the other Priestesses to enjoy their evening meal. Something she had been skipping to be with Alexeii; instead, she enjoyed bread and cheeses from the kitchen on her return. Tonight he was being called to a neighbouring City to discuss his next battle. Before that, Cora hadn't thought of him leaving. Not allowing herself to believe that they wouldn't see each other every day. Her heart already breaking at the thought of him at war. Knowing he was a skilled Warrior wasn't enough to ease her mind.

Sitting with her Sisters, eating together and chatting about their day took her mind off thinking about Alexeii's imminent departure. Still catching Helia's intense eyes trying to find answers, she laughed at one of the other Priestesses stories of nearly catching her ceremonial gowns on fire during their last ceremony and how the Goddess was 'heating things up' for them all.

When the conversation moved round to initiations, Cora became unsettled. This was not a topic she wanted to discuss, especially around Helia. Making her excuses that she needed to do some journaling, she left the table and made her way to her chambers.

"Cora, wait!" Phoebe ran up behind her. Grabbing her hand, asking if Cora would braid her hair.

"I was just about to do some journaling, but yes, let's go to your chambers. You have your ribbons?"

"Yes, I made some today out of old cloths."

"Brilliant." Together they walked hand in hand to Phoebe's chambers. Her light chatter accompanying them all the way.

For the next hour, Cora braided Phoebe's hair and listened, once again to her chat about patrons. How she imagined it to be. Did Cora remember her first one? Stuttering, she replied she did, trying to divert the subject away once more.

"What is it Cora? Where you scared? Did you do it wrong?" Thinking that Cora's hesitance was because of a bad memory, Phoebe probed her for more information. Her own fears of what it may be like, thick in her eyes.

"Not at all. It was quite beautiful. I surrendered completely to the Goddess and followed her lead. There really isn't anything to worry about Phoebe. All your training beforehand will ensure you are more than ready." Hoping that would put Phoebe's mind to rest, Cora yawned and stretched. Letting her know that she was tired now and would be heading back to her chambers to sleep.

It would be an early rise for Cora in the morning to see Alexeii, dreading to hear about his imminent departure yet dying to be with him.

Entering the warm chambers, she found Helia sat writing. Cora's entrance had turned her attention away from her journal to her distant Sister. "I thought you were journaling also this evening?"

Quickly the once warm room started to feel cold.

Shivering from Helia's frosty stare, Cora replied, "Ah yes, I met Phoebe in the halls and she begged me to braid her hair, which of course resulted in many questions about coming of age ceremonies" Cora giggled, trying to bring a lightness to their conversation.

"I can imagine, Sibyl is exactly the same." Both women spent a little time swapping stories about their wards before Cora got into bed and wished her Sister good night. Proclaiming that she was exhausted and would be up before dawn the next day.

Just as she was nodding off, Helia asked, "Are you all right Cora? I'm worried about you."

Not wanting to get into much of a conversation, she simply replied, "Yes, I am. Just working things through, you know how it is with initiations." Turning over to face away from Helia, she hoped that would be the end of the questions for one day.

Cora woke to the sound of songbirds from her window, dawn was breaking and it was time to see Alexeii. At the pit of her stomach, heaviness alerted her to the awkward conversation she knew she would be having with him. He would be leaving her to return to war; it was just a matter of when - the thought of not seeing him weighed heavy on her heart. Quietly getting dressed so as not to disturb Helia, she left to meet her love - worries of what he might share consumed her as she left the Temple towards the forest, not realising that there was someone else who was up early that morning.

Phoebe was coming around the side of the Temple towards the labyrinth and just caught sight of Cora heading towards the forest. Awake at this time to journey with her thoughts and questions through the labyrinth, she decided she would look for Cora after her short ceremony as she had a dream through the night that had unsettled her.

Finally reaching the Cypress tree, Cora was surprised that Alexeii wasn't there to greet her. Instantly fearful that he wouldn't return to her, already being called to war. Tears sprung in her eyes. Sitting under the shade of her favourite tree, she wept. The loss of him was heartbreaking. *Will I see him again?* Remembering their last time together, his sweet kisses and gentle touch. Already missing him.

"Cora?" She hadn't heard him approach. Looking up at his beautiful face, leaping up to wrap herself around him, she kissed every inch of his face.

"Oh, morning to you too! What's happening, are you well?"

"Yes! Yes! When you weren't here, I thought you had left for war. I didn't think I would see you again!" The joy of being in his arms was overwhelming. She never wanted to be anywhere else other than here.

"Oh sweetheart, I am so sorry. I slept in a little after a long night talking and drinking with some of my men as we put some plans in place. I didn't mean for you to worry". Scooping her up into his arms, nestling her into his neck, he soothed her.

"I never want to be without you Alexeii. I love you."

"I love you too, sweet Cora. We will find a way; love always does." Neither could believe the power and passion of their mutual affection for each other in such a short time. Their souls instantly knowing they belonged together.

Cradling her into his chest, he laid down under the tree. Loving the moment of being with the other as the birds sang and leaves gently rustled above their heads. Cora's knew she had to ask.

"Will you be leaving for war soon?"

"We had a long conversation last night. It would seem that the battles are small right now and my men are handling them well. It hasn't been an easy task defending our lands; however, things seem fairly settled for now." Searching Cora's eyes, he could see her relief. It warmed his heart to know that she wanted him near.

"So you are staying?"

"For now at least, probably for the next few months as long as there are no serious invasions." Heart leaping once more, she reached up, circling hands around his neck, pulling him down to her. Placing urgent kisses upon his mouth, she opened to devour him. The words he spoke fuelling her passion as they tore at each other's clothing.

Desire rose in Cora as she began to move beneath him. Her sex wanting his attention, thrusting towards him. Fingers tracing his lips where her mouth had left them red and swollen. Feeling his heartbeat loud in his chest as she moved her fingers downwards. Slow and seductive, she let her fingers linger over his tight nipples, biting her lip in anticipation of his own desire being unleashed upon her.

Watching her was intoxicating. Her eyes shining with lust and love. It took all his strength to hold back, to witness her tease and play. Seeing her own nipples tighten as they brushed his chest brought a rush of heat to his sex. Those eyes! Intense with desire, they shone like the sun on the blue seas. Moving strands of golden hair behind her ear, he lay gentle kisses on her bare shoulder and up her neck, feeling her shudder with pleasure with each feather-light touch.

Shifting positions, Cora moved on top of Alexeii. Laying her whole body on his, his arms snaking around her waist as their lips locked in a passionate kiss. Moving slowly to kiss his neck, chest, slithering down his body to lay lips on his torso, feeling him ripple with desire beneath her touch. His hardness calling to her, wanting to taste him, Cora let her tongue guide her. Holding him at his base, fingers laced around his wanting sex.

Gazing up at him, she smiled seductively as she let her tongue circle his tip, licking up the droplets of his arousal. Gasping with the intensity of the feelings he was experiencing at her touch, he weaved his fingers through her hair, allowing his head to fall back and his pelvis to thrust forward as she took him fully in her mouth.

Taking him to the edge of ecstasy over and over with tongue and mouth, slowing down when she knew he was nearing release. Letting the sensations ebb and flow, over and over again. She loved the sounds he made, how his hands felt in her hair, holding her gently but firmly over his sex. Feeling the intensity of their connection deepen.

Knowing she needed to feel him inside her, Cora moved back up his body, finding his lips once more. His need for her growing as he could taste his own essence on her tongue, to be one with her, moved him into action. Shifting their positions, her now below his body, looking intensely into her eyes, he guided his sex to her opening. Gently circling around and over her bulging clitoris. Her juices flowing for him. Slowly he entered inside of her, every inch of him being welcomed by her inner Temple.

Locked in each other's pleasure, neither noticed they were being watched. Shocked at the sight of tangled naked bodies in the distance, Phoebe stood frozen at the edge of the meadow. Her search for Cora in the forest led her here, a place she knew Cora loved to collect medicinal flowers for anointing oils. Noticing movement hidden behind the high grasses near a Cypress tree, Phoebe's eyes focused in to see how they moved rhythmically with the meadow flowers. If she hadn't been searching for Cora, she probably would never have noticed them.

Inching closer, fascinated at witnessing such erotic passion, Phoebe held her breath, not wanting to disturb the lovers but her childlike curiosity needing to see more. He was on top of her. All she saw of her was her shapely thighs folded around his hips. The closer she got, she could feel their hot passion. It excited her to see such things. Knowing the blessing of pleasure.

Kneeling down in the grasses so she could keep hidden yet still see what was happening from a distance, Phoebe knew she probably shouldn't be there. Intrigue now masked with knowing that this was a sacred act and she should leave them be. Just as she was about to quietly move away, she saw a flash of golden hair as the woman raised herself on top of him.

Knowing only one person with such unusual colouring, her eyes were now transfixed. Hair covering her face she couldn't quite see, *surely it couldn't be?* Waiting to glimpse her face from beneath the veil of golden strands, already instinctively knowing who it was.

Phoebe stared at the lovers and got the confirmation she needed. *It was Cora. Her Priestess, making love to a man in the meadow's, outwith the Temple.* Shocked, she took flight back through the forest she needed to get back. Not sure what to do or think, heart racing in her chest, she ran straight into Helia.

"Phoebe! Where are you going in such a hurry?"

Relieved to see Helia, she needed to confide in someone about what she saw. Not being able to trust the other Melissae, she blurted out.

"I just saw Cora in the meadow, laying with a man, naked".

"What? Our Cora? What man? When?" Shock raising Helia's voice, she demanded of Phoebe to tell her more.

Breathlessly Phoebe divulged, "I was searching for Cora to talk to her and I saw movement at the edge of the meadow behind the forest under a Cypress tree. I saw it was naked bodies and... I know I shouldn't have. I'm sorry Helia." Phoebe burst into tears, afraid that she had done something wrong.

"It's all right Phoebe, you're not in any trouble. Tell me exactly what you saw."

"It was a man making love to a woman. I couldn't see the woman; she lay beneath him. I moved a little closer and then I saw her move on top of him. It was the hair Helia, golden hair. I knew it could only be Cora and then I saw her face. It was her! Oh Helia, I'm so sorry. I shouldn't have been there. I didn't know you could see patron's outside of the Temple. Was it a special ceremony? I got such a fright!" Crying, she lunged her head into Helia's chest. Stroking Phoebe's auburn hair, an array of emotions and thoughts ran through her mind.

What was Cora doing with a man? Who was it? Is that what she had been doing all this time? It was inconceivable to Helia that Cora would sneak off for weeks now to be with a man. *Surely she would have confided in her, would she not? Why hadn't she known?*

Her cheeks reddened as she was filled with hurt, anger and fear for Cora. Knowing what must be done, Helia left the temple grounds. Speaking her truth was imperative here to protect Cora; she would need to confront it head-on. Tears streaming down her face at the feelings of betrayal that her best friend and Sister hadn't confided in her and she had to learn the truth from Phoebe stung her heart. All those early mornings and nights, worrying that she was alone, to find out she was sneaking away with a man! Doing what she knew was best, straight-talking was the only way to ensure Cora was safe. Arriving in front of the door of the chamber, she took a deep breath and entered.

"Helia! You startled me. I didn't hear you knock!"

"I'm sorry High Priestess, I have something urgent I must tell you."

Chapter 10

Seeing the look of distraught in Helia's eyes, Ophelia knew it was about Cora.

"What has happened Helia?"

Unsure of where to start, Helia stumbled over her words. "She was seen in the meadow with a man. Phoebe saw her there naked with him!"

Ophelia had known that Cora's continued disappearance from the Temple most mornings and nights meant that she was meeting with someone. Hoping that it wasn't a love interest and perhaps, as Cora had said, she was meeting with the Goddess, it didn't come as a huge shock to hear this, although she was disappointed that she had chosen to hide it.

"Do we know who the man is?"

Bursting into tears, Helia shook her head. The pain of knowing that Cora had been hiding this from her was excruciating.

"No, I had no idea High Priestess. How could she have kept this from me? Most mornings and evenings she leaves the Temple, telling me that she was journaling and moving through her initiation. I even shared with her about the affections from my own patron and she said nothing!"

Understanding the feelings of betrayal that left tear marks down Helia's face, Ophelia embraced her.

"I will need to speak to her. Do we know anything more than what Phoebe saw?"

"I know nothing other than Phoebe saw her making love to a man at the meadow behind the forest." Deflated, Helia slipped from Ophelia's embrace and sat upon the furs on the floor. The full realisation hit her hard. Cora had been lying to her face this whole time.

* * *

Skipping back through the forest, her heart light after spending a sensual morning with Alexeii knowing that he wouldn't be leaving any time soon, Cora marvelled at how blessed she was by the Goddess to have a love such as he. Colour rushing to her cheeks as she remembered the way she had moved upon him, taking his full manhood within her. Seeing his eyes looking up at her with so much love, his hands running over her breasts as they moved rhythmically together. His pleasure rippling inside of her as she soon experienced her own.

Suddenly remembering that she would have to collect some more silphium - to soak in cotton to ensure she wouldn't get with child. Glad of her Priestess training that educated her on the herbs she needed as a sexual priestess to ensure his seed wouldn't impregnate her.

Mind-wandering, she didn't notice Helia's ward, Sibyl running towards her.

"Cora! Cora!" Her attention caught by the urgency in her voice, Cora ran to Sibyl.

"What is it? What has happened?"

"Our High Priestess needs to see you right away. She asked me to bring you straight to her."

Startled by Sibyl's words, Cora took flight with her towards the Temple. Concerned that something was wrong, she worried that Helia may be unwell or the High Priestess herself.

Out of breath, Cora knocked on Ophelia's door. On her reply to enter, Cora took one look at Ophelia's face and seeing Helia sitting forlornly on the floor, she rushed to her, believing that her friend was unwell.

"What has happened? Are you hurt?" Searching Helia's face to see if she was harmed, Cora was shocked to see those intense hazel eyes now filled with such rage.

"How could you? How could you lie to me all this time?" Helia spat.

Pulling back, Cora was confused with the outburst of rage projected towards her.

"What do you mean? Tell me what has happened?" Fear building in Cora as the realisation hit her that perhaps she knew about Alexeii.

"You were seen Cora. At the meadow, naked with a man. Is this what you have been doing morning and night when you said to me you just needed to be alone! Have you been hiding this from me!" Helia's voice rose to a shriek, unable to hide her disgust at what Cora had done to her.

Blood rushing to Cora's face as the accusation of being a liar hit home.

Stuttering, Cora couldn't get the words out. Deep down, she knew that she would be found out, although she was the one to frequent the meadow every day to collect the herbs, others would go there to rest and sometimes play. She hadn't been careful enough. Now they all knew the truth.

"Helia, go fetch some water; I need to speak to Cora alone." Ophelia instructed.

Stomping out of the room without even a glance at Cora, Helia left, slamming the door behind her. Never before had she seen Helia in this way. So much anger. Realising how hurt she must be, Cora looked hesitantly at Ophelia, awaiting her wrath.

"I am not angry Cora. I am disappointed. I need you to tell me who this man is and how long it has been going on. I believed we had honesty between us and I know Helia certainly thought you had that between you both also. You have not only been laying with a man for weeks now, but you have also continued to lie to us all, that hurts Cora."

Shame flaming her cheeks, Cora began to cry. Never wanting to hurt her Sisters, lost in her own lust and love for Alexeii., she didn't really know where to start, nor did she want to divulge her sacred moments with him.

"Who is he Cora? Was he a patron?"

"Yes. He was my very first patron." Eyes focused on the floor, Cora heard Ophelia's deep intake of breath.

"What do you mean? You have been seeing him this whole time?"

"No, no High Priestess. He came back to the Temple weeks ago. I recognised him straight away. I love him..." The words dripped from her mouth. Unsure of where they would land with Ophelia or if she could even understand.

"You know our ways Cora. Our patrons do not lay with us. They are not pleasured by us; they are the patrons of the Goddess. She works through us. Yes, there is love, devotion, worship, pleasure, but it is not ours personally. You know this, how has it moved beyond our Temple walls?" Demanding more information Cora could feel herself freeze up. Wanting to defend her love for him. It was not the Goddess' love; it was hers.

"It just did! That second encounter was like no other. The Goddess left us alone. I do love him and he loves me. The Goddess has gifted this to us both. I cannot explain it. I just know it exists. I don't expect you to understand." Spitting those last words to Ophelia opened a wound that had never quite healed within her.

"I wouldn't understand? How is that so Cora? I have been a Priestess for decades; I know love through the Goddess and personally. Our surrender to it, to Her, to our Temple lives, that makes us who we are. You cannot be a Temple Priestess and share your love and devotion, outwith these walls. You already know this. You will not be able to see him again."

Knowing the truth of being a Priestess and accepting her fate that she would not see Alexeii again broke something within Cora. Fleeing from the room in tears, she ran back towards the forest. Needing to get as far away from Ophelia and her life as a Priestess as she could.

How could she say those things? How could I be without my love? It was not possible. I will not! Not knowing where to turn or what she could do, Cora sat in the forest alone. She wasn't able to go to Alexeii. Not knowing where he stayed. Helia's rage for her meant she couldn't go to her either. Feeling sick to her stomach, thinking of Ophelia's demands to not see him again. Sobs rattled through her, never had she felt so alone as she did now.

* * *

Pacing the room, seething, Helia waited for Cora to return to their chambers. Needing to know the truth, to find out how far she had gone with her lies. Still, Helia had no idea who this man was or how long it had been going on. The tears from earlier leaving her eyes puffy and red, irritation of being asked to leave Ophelia's chambers when all she wanted to do was confront Cora, had her skin boiling.

She wasn't going to wait a minute longer. Storming out of the room, she walked straight into Sibyl and Phoebe, who had been waiting outside, wondering whether or not they should see if Helia was all right.

"Girls, what are you doing?"

"We just wanted to make sure you were well? We saw how upset you were when you left the High Priestess' chambers". The girls looked at each other nervously, unsure now if they should have just left Helia alone.

"I'm fine. Do you know where Cora is? Is she still with our High Priestess?" Urgent to confront her, not caring if she was still with Ophelia, she was going to have her say.

"No, she left. We saw her heading towards the forest while we were in the gardens."

Another flush of hot rage ran through Helia, shouting thanks behind her as she took off at full speed for the forest, heart racing as her feet pounded the ground, wind stinging her face as tears streamed down her cheeks.

Stopping suddenly, Healia saw Cora curled up under a tree, a flash of concern that she was hurt, which was quickly replaced with anger as she abruptly said her name.

Startled, Cora awoke from her restless sleep, "Helia?"

"We need to talk." Helia spat, unable to hold back her distaste for what her closest friend had done.

"Yes. I'm so sorry Helia. I'm sorry I never told you."

"Who is he Cora? Where is he from? How long?" Firing questions that had been churning around since Phoebe first told her, Helia could feel the betrayal come spilling out.

Resigning to telling Helia everything, a sense of relief to finally be able to share mixed with the fear that she too would demand her not to see him again.

"His name is Alexeii. He was my first patron who returned around six weeks ago. I love him Helia."

Thinking that knowing the truth would give her some relief, Helia found herself even more angered. *Six weeks! Without a word from Cora that she had been seeing him. Now she loved him?*

"How Cora? How can you love him? How could you keep this from me all this time? You know our ways. You know it is forbidden! How could you Cora?" Her voice rising to a shriek again, in all these years, Cora had never seen her Sister so enraged.

"Helia, you don't understand. He was gifted to me by the Goddess. My soul mate. I am so sorry I never told you; I was scared. I know it is forbidden, but the energy between us, Helia the love, it is Divine."

"So 'Divine' that you hide it? Sneak away each morning and night to see him, weeks on end. Lie to my face, to our High Priestess? You told me you wanted to be alone! That is not Divinity Cora. It is betrayal. It is wrong." The weight of her words hit Cora directly in her heart.

Tears streaming from her eyes, she begged Helia to forgive her. Needing her Sister to understand but knowing she never would.

"I don't know what else to say Helia. I need to be with him. If I am made to leave him, I know my heart will split in two. He is everything to me."

"More than our Goddess? More than our High Priestess? More than me?" Searching Cora's eyes, scared that she would see that he did indeed mean more to her than she. *Had this stranger placed some kind of spell on her? Manifesting Cora would leave all she has known for ten years to be with a man she has only known for six weeks!*

Not waiting on a response, Helia looked Cora directly in her eyes and said, "He has to go Cora. You can't have both!" With that, she turned away and walked back to the Temple. Hearing the sobs from her Sister as she went, hoping that she would indeed choose her.

Chapter 11

"You will not see him again Cora, if you wish to stay here. You will also have to move through the Priestess rituals of cleansing and worship again before you can be of full service to the Goddess with her patrons. Also…"

Ophelia softened her tone to say the following words, knowing they would sting Cora's heart. "Helia has requested that you no longer share a bed chamber. She has moved into chambers with her Sister Iris; this will give you space to work through what is happening for you Cora."

Cora's heart broke. Losing her love and her best friend felt like a harsh punishment. *Why would the Goddess give so abundantly then rip it all away so cruelly?* The pain of being forbidden to see Alexeii again, not even to say goodbye or explain to him, was excruciating.

She imagined him waiting at their tree for her, not knowing why she wasn't there. Tears seemed to be running down her face continually, her throat raw. Wishing she hadn't returned from the forest - instead, had run to the village searching for Alexeii, knowing she would thump on every door to find him. But no, she had chosen to return to the Temple, in the naive hope that they would see her pain, understand her need to be with him.

What she had received was more pain and hurt, no understanding and complete rejection of her heart. Unsure of how she would move forward, being stripped away of her Priestess duties and instead hauled back to her initial training, Cora lost herself in her thoughts. *Why is the Goddess punishing me? Why did I not run from all of this?*

The Melissae and other Priestesses were instructed to keep a close eye on Cora. She was not permitted to leave the Temple, even into the gardens unless chaperoned. What once felt like home now felt like a prison. No longer able to pick herbs and flowers from the meadow or watch the moonlight glisten through the forest ceiling. Instead, her freedom had been stolen from her.

Most nights, she fell asleep with hot tears upon her face, angered at the Goddess, Ophelia and Helia for their betrayal to her heart. Hours spent wondering where her Alexeii could be. So scared that he had come to the Temple only to be turned away - or worse, he hadn't come at all.

It didn't matter where Cora was, helping ready her Priestess sisters at the ritual baths for their day with their patrons or at the altars in prayer and worship; eyes were always on her. Stripping her rights for love away with each stare. Spending most of her time within her bed chambers, being free of the eyes, was the only place Cora felt safe.

Helia hadn't spoken to her in the few weeks since her heated words in the forest. That loss created a gaping hole in Cora's heart. No one to talk to each evening, no one to spend time with, knowing that she had hurt her dearest friend by keeping her love for Alexeii secret, but still shocked that Helia hadn't tried to resolve their issues as she had. Many times she had knocked on her chamber door, only to be faced with a forlorn looking Iris, shaking her head as she relayed the message that Helia didn't want to see her. *How long before she would forgive her? Would she ever?*

Days were long, nights even longer. Often waking up covered in a sweat, thinking she heard the shouts of Alexeii calling her to him. Lying awake for hours after fantasising about being with him, his hands on her body, his mouth on hers. Torturing herself as she got lost in memories of their lovemaking. The pain ripping open her heart once more.

Why Persephone? Why has this been my initiation? To love so deeply and then for it all to be ripped away? Have I angered you? Betrayed you? What must I do to show you my devotion? What must I do to have my love and Sister return to me?

Plea after plea and yet nothing, no answers came from the Goddess. Her questions only met with silence. Sitting at the foot of her altar for hours - begging to hear her, speak with her to no avail. The Goddess had turned her back on her, for that she was sure.

Weeks ran into months, the pain of loss never ceasing, the memory of Alexeii never fading; however, her full Priestess service was to return. Moving through the Priestess rites and rituals once more, it was time to be with the Goddess' patrons again.

Secretly hoping that Alexeii would be the next one to walk through the door, deep down knowing that was impossible, Cora did what was asked of her. She performed her duties in dedication to a Goddess that would embody her but not converse with her.

Moving through the sacred ceremony, bringing pleasure and passion to those she was of service to, going through the motions and surrendering to the Goddess. Allowing Her to lead. Always keeping herself locked away, not engaging in the unity that she once felt so connected to.

Looking at the man who lay spent under soft furs laid on the chamber floor, Cora rang the bell for the Melissae to enter. Longing for the spark of energy to return to her after being with a patron. That electric bolt that she used to revel in once a ceremony was over, how she loved feeling pleasure move through her for the rest of the day. Cora longed to be at one with the Goddess, giving up hope of ever feeling the passion and joy of laying with Alexeii again.

As she left the chambers, Phoebe greeted her. "High Priestess would like to see you in her chambers. Are you well Cora? You look drained Sister?" Usually, it was lovely to see the Priestesses after being in ceremony with their patron, glowing and pulsating with joy. It was unusual to see such deflation that Phoebe saw in Cora.

"Yes, I am fine Phoebe, just tired. I will go to her now."

"Would you like me to accompany you?" Hoping that Cora would say yes so she could help to bring her energies up again, a knack the young Melissae had as part of her healing abilities.

"Thank you Phoebe, but no. I'm sure you have more pressing duties to be getting on with". Nodding, Phoebe left

Cora to walk away, silently worrying that the light she loved so much in her older Sister would never fully return.

Knocking on Ophelia's door, she opened it, seeing her face, she knew there was something wrong. "You called for me High Priestess?"

"Yes Cora. How are you finding your time with your patrons? Is the Goddess with you?" Searching eyes moved over Cora's face. Knowing Ophelia was reading her, now more intensely than ever before. Since she had deceived Ophelia, she often had to face her intense gaze, reaching into her psyche to see whether or not she was speaking the truth.

"Yes, she is with me. I feel her enter me, lead me. I am following our Sacred rituals with my patrons. Why do you ask?"

"To be honest Cora, we have had some complaints from your patrons. They often say that they experience the energy during your time together, but most have found that their crops are now dying, or their business is drying up. When it first started to happen, I thought it was just a disgruntled patron. Now it seems a week or so after being in ceremony with you, they are experiencing significant losses."

"Oh." Although it shocked Cora to hear what Ophelia had shared with her, knowing this happens in other Temple's, Cora intuitively knew that her pain and loss must be transferring to her patrons. Again, asking the Goddess *why this was happening* and more so, why she *was allowing it to happen?*

"I'm not sure what to say. I am doing the ceremony as I have always done. The Goddess is there with me, working through me."

"There is a sadness in you Cora. I don't think you realise how powerful a Priestess you are. The pain you are carrying is so potent it is transferring to your patrons, even with the Goddess working through you." Ophelia's voice softened. Realising how much Cora was hurting, believing that she would have overcome the grief of losing her lover by now. Remembering how her own heart had started to heal and it never transferred on to her patrons.

"I don't know what to do High Priestess. I have gone through all the rituals. I have completed many healing ceremonies. I try to forget him, but my heart won't. It longs for him day and night. I often wake to hear him call for me, but he has not returned and I cannot go to him. I'm trying High Priestess..."

Her eyes welling up, she stared at the floor. Believing that this pain would never go, learning how to live with it. She often prayed to the Goddess to forget him and heal her heart, but it just ripped off the scabs, the pain of not being with him soaring through her once more.

"I hear you Sister. I have witnessed how much effort you have put into your healing. Each day I pray to our Goddess for you to find peace, only to see your pain etched deeper..."

Ophelia was silent as she searched for the answer. Seeing Cora in front of her now, a poor reflection of the vibrant woman she once knew. Her heart knew what needed to be said, but her fears were making it hard to say the words.

"I have been where you are before Cora. I have loved a man too." Hearing the vulnerability in Ophelia's voice Cora gasped.

"You have known love? Outwith the Temple?"

"Yes. A long time ago, before you came here. I fell deeply in love with a man, not a patron, a man who was working the land close by."

The memory of him tore at Ophelia's heart. For years she had pushed it down far enough that the pain of leaving him wasn't a constant reminder.

"How do you live with the pain? Does it ever go away?" Cora pleaded, desperate to be rid of the tearing of her heart that never seemed to heal.

"It never truly goes away, but the harshness of it does soften. My dedication to the Goddess, our work here in the Temple was the healing balm I needed."

"How long did it take? How long before I feel the relief? I'm not sure I can go on any more, especially if my service is causing pain to my patron's. What is left for me here?"

Seeing how distraught Cora was, Ophelia knew what she had to do. "Cora, there is something I must tell you. We have been keeping it from you, hoping that it would help in your healing and that you could forget and move forward. Praying the Goddess would ease your pain and your service to her and the Temple would ease your mind."

Staring at Ophelia, Cora waited for her to divulge what they had been hiding from her.

"He has been here. Every day - morning and night. He sleeps in the forest. Every morning he begs to see you, often with a message he wants us to give to you. Each night he comes to the Temple door, leaving gifts for the Goddess, hoping that she will allow his entry to be with you as Her patron. It is his voice you hear calling out your name Cora."

Not sure whether to yell in anger or joy, Cora let Ophelia's words sink in. *He was still here after all this time? Alexeii wanted to be with me still?*

"I must go to him. I need to see him. Speak to him." Grabbing Cora's arm as she started to run for the door, Ophelia spun her round to look intently into her eyes.

"If you go to him, you will not be able to say goodbye. Cora, if you go to him now, you will not be able to return to the Temple." Ophelia's words, although spoken softly, were a sharp blow to Cora.

"What do you mean I won't be able to return?"

"You know our ways Cora. To be a Priestess is to worship only to Her, to serve Her. No man would allow you to continue your work here with the patron's and be with him. You know that you cannot live here with a man. It is forbidden. If you go to him now Cora, you will not be able to leave him and in doing so, you will be leaving us."

The ultimatum her High Priestess laid upon her shoulders sealed her fate. No, she could not live without him. Her soul-deep love for him meant that it would never be possible, not now she knew he wanted her.

Running from the room, Cora fled through the Temple, not thinking that it would be the last time she would ever be within its walls. Leaving behind her Sisters, her Priestesshood, her Temple life, she ran to the forest, shouting Alexeii's name. Never again would she be without him.

Knowing that he had waited for her, begged to see her each day and night. It was all she needed to know to give in to the pull in her heart to be in his arms once more.

"Alexeii! Alexeii! Where are you?" Shouting his name, calling out to him to return to her, she heard his faint cry in the distance.

"Cora?" Heart beating in his chest Alexeii wondered if his mind was playing tricks on him. Was it her calling to him? Jumping to his feet, he ran towards her voice. Leaping over fallen branches, his initial hesitance released to the need to find her, be with her.

Glimpsing her from a distance, momentarily, his heart stopped. It was her! The love of his life, she who he never thought he would see again, running towards him, calling to him. Tears rushed to his eyes as he closed the gap between them. Finally, they embraced, sweeping her around him in pure joy. Laying kisses all over her tear-streaked face, at last, she had returned!

Chapter 12

The heat between them was instant. Weeks apart had left their hearts torn, but now, on their reunion, they were whole again.

"I have missed you so much Alexeii, I only just found out that you were coming to the Temple every day. I am so sorry."

In between sweet kisses, he replied, "Do not worry Cora. I am just so happy you are here." Staring intently into her eyes, still not quite believing she was in his arms once more. Sweeping a golden strand off her face, he leant in to deepen his kiss with hers. Locking in passion, they momentarily forgot about their pain. Being with each other was all that mattered.

Feeling the heat rise from within her, Cora let out a gentle moan of pure delight. To be with him was to be home. Forgetting that she now no longer had a physical home, the Temple doors now closed to her, Cora enjoyed the moment of delicious kisses from her love.

Their urgency began to rise, "Let's go to our tree Cora, I want to move away from this forest. It has been my prison these last weeks. Scared to leave it in case you returned but feeling trapped at the same time."

"I am so sorry Alexeii..." Walking out of the forest towards their Cypress tree, Cora explained to Alexeii what had happened. How Helia had gone to Ophelia when she found out about them. Ophelia's demands placed upon her to never see him again. She shared those weeks of pure torture and even what had been happening with her patrons. "I tried to forget you Alexeii, but my heart never could."

Her words stung. He knew it was impossible to ever forget her, becoming aware of that many years before, when he first met her as her patron.

"There is something between us Cora. Something I have always felt but never truly understood until now. You are my soul mate. I want to build a life with you. To be together completely." Holding her to him as they walked, feeling her hot tears drip on his arm. Looking down at her, as she looked up into his eyes, they both knew what he said was their truth, even if no one else could understand.

Laying her down beneath the shadow of the Cypress leaves, Alexeii took a moment to take her in. Seeing her here now in the moonlight, he wondered if she was a mirage. Had he finally drove himself crazy enough that his fantasies of laying with her again had become so life like?

"Come to me..." Her words shifted him out of his worries. She was real. Finally, they were together again. Whatever happened to bring her to him, he would find out later. For now, they were deep diving into their love for each other.

Undressing her slowly, he relished in the feeling of her warm, voluptuous body. Seeing the moonlight once more bounce off her skin. Never tiring of the sight of his Goddess illuminating his World. Feeling her fingers reach for him, pulling at his belt to remove his tunic.

Staring intently, his thickset body standing above her as he removed his tunic, the darkness of his hair curled around his chest, his manhood. Yes, he wanted her; that was clear for her to see. His phallus thick and hard for her. Longing to feel it inside of her own Sacred Temple. To become one with him once more.

Reaching up, she pulled him down to her. Instantly a fire was released from within. Hands moving over his chest, up to his strong jaw, curling around the back of his neck as she opened her mouth to receive his tongue. His hands cupping her breasts, thumb circling her erect nipple. Feeling his erection against her thigh, moving her hands to hold him, curling fingers around his sex, hearing his intake of breath as she gently squeezed.

Her soul drawing him in. Legs instinctively beginning to spread as his fingers traced over her opening. Pulsating over her pleasure point as ecstasy rippled through her body. Feeling his way inside of her, entering her inner sacred space, exploring her folds, her own fingers moving rhythmically over his hardened sex.

Both feeling the rise of their Sexual energy, calling for them to unite as one. Moving from Cora's side to lay between her legs, Alexeii connected with her soul through her eyes as he entered her. Their divine connection made. No longer separate, now as one.

Tears spilt from her eyes with complete joy. This man within her was her World. Love exploding from her heart into every cell of her Being. Fireworks of pleasure bursting from head to toe. Seeing in his eyes pure love and joy as they moved together, seeking more.

His release was earth-shattering. Ecstasy was theirs as their climax moved in waves throughout their body. Pure love swelled in his heart as he moved to lay by her side, deliciously spent as they lay in each other's arms under the light of the moon.

It didn't matter what had happened before or what was to come; right now, they were together in love. Everything else could be worked out.

Reaching over to pull his robes over them both, allowing the ground below to be their bed, they fell into a deep sleep, both exhausted with weeks of pain and unrest. Feeling safe in the other's arms, they knew now that they could never be parted.

* * *

Leaving the Temple with nothing but the robes on her back was difficult for Cora to contemplate her future. Alexeii had taken her to his home, one he had bought within the first week of their meeting. Knowing no matter where he was to go as a warrior, home would always be where she was.

Never allowing himself to believe that she would live with him, knowing that her life as a Priestess was who she was, it amazed Alexeii to see her there. In his bed, their bed now. Spending evenings in the courtyard, eating together. It was indeed a dream come true.

Cora was grateful that his home was on the edge of the village, already knowing from their brief trips to purchase clothing, she was being talked about. Standing out as she did with her opal skin and golden locks. *Who was she? Where had she come from? I'm sure she is one of the Priestesses? Why had she left the Temple?* Whispers that followed her wherever she went.

Of course, she was happy to be with Alexeii, never quite believing that she would be living with him, laying with him every night. But her whole adult life had involved being a Priestess and now that was over. She cried some nights, missing her Sisters, the Temple and even her patrons. The work she did was part of who she was.

Alexeii was always understanding, making sure that this was what she truly wanted. Letting her know that he would support her if she wanted to return. No, that was not an option, not if it meant not being with him. Her life was here, in his arms. Being without him was impossible and she couldn't have both. It was forbidden to be a Priestess and live with your lover.

Cora filled her days planting in their courtyard, the herbs she loved and missed. Adding touches to their home to make it theirs. They often cooked together, marvelling at how wonderful Alexeii was as she remembered the men in her own childhood home. Never lifting a hand to help the women.

"Why do you cook with me Alexeii? When I was young, the men never came near the kitchen."

"I am a warrior Cora. I have lived alone or in camps with other men most of my life. If we didn't cook, we didn't eat. Also, I love spending time with you, creating together." Pulling her in for a warm embrace, so grateful that he could.

Something lingered at the back of Cora's mind. A conversation a few months ago about Alexeii next leaving for war in four months. Knowing that they both knew that time was coming, but not daring to speak the words.

It only took Cora a few weeks to make a home from the house that Alexeii bought. The newly planted herbs were already sprouting, the living area filled with vibrant colours from the fabric she had purchased in the village. She even created an altar and placed the beautiful marble carving of the Goddess that Alexeii had already purchased before leaving the Temple. Saying that he prayed to Her every day to bring Cora to him.

She kept busy with her daily self rituals, cooking and lovemaking. Something she would never tire of. Many a night, she would feel his hand reach out for hers and before they knew it, their legs would be tangled together, sweat beading on their bodies after another night of pleasure.

Or better still, he would come behind her while she kneaded bread, lacing his arms around her waist, pulling her to his chest. Hours later, they would find themselves exhausted from pleasuring each other. On one of these occasions, Cora found herself asking the question they had both kept silent about.

"Months ago, you told me that you may have to return to war. Alexeii, when will this be?"

Uncomfortably he moved away from her. Reaching for his robe, he tied it around his waist. Searching for the words that he knew would hurt them both.

"Two weeks Cora. I have to return in two weeks." Seeing shock in her eyes at how soon four months had come around, he lay beside her again, pulling her to his chest.

"So soon. How long will you be gone?" Dreading the answer, she braced herself for his reply.

"It could be anything between four to six months..."

"That long? Oh Alexeii, what will we do?" Already feeling the pain of their separation strangling her, Cora shifted away from him.

"I can hopefully return each month for a day or so to be with you Cora. I wish I could stay with you forever. But I am needed by my men. I have a duty as a warrior."

Feeling the pang of remembrance of her own promise as a Priestess and how she had left that life to be with him, she spat back. "I'm well aware of that duty Alexeii. I had made my own promises which I left behind to be with you."

"I know you have, for that, I am so very sorry. If I don't go, our lands will be ravaged. Trust me Cora, I have thought of how I could stay. I have even looked for work close to home. The truth is, this calling has been with me since birth. I need to protect. If I don't and something happened to you, I would never forgive myself."

Softening to his words, knowing that part of him was what she fell in love with, she allowed herself to see it from his perspective, even though she wished with all her might that it wasn't so.

* * *

The days flew by, preparing Alexeii for war, spending as much time with each other as possible. Planning what they would do on his days when he returned. Alexeii ensuring she had everything she needed while he was away.

He had purchased a spinning wheel and some tools to create her own pottery. Knowing how much she loved to make beautiful things. Helping her to plan how she would spend her days.

It filled Cora's heart to see how hard he was trying to help her. Of course, she would enjoy spinning and creating her own pottery, but it wouldn't fill the hole in her heart that his time away from her would create. Instead, she focused on when she would see him again.

The night before his departure Cora set up a whole ceremony for him. With cleansing baths, healing oils and calling in the Goddess during their lovemaking, all to ensure his safety and triumph at war.

Feeling blessed to know her life as a Priestess could still hold power even though she was no longer in the Temple, comforted her. Knowing she would do rituals every day to ensure his safe return helped her feel empowered in a situation she couldn't control.

Praying the night would go on forever, knowing daylight would bring his departure, she curled up close to him. Sleep would not be theirs for that one night as he held her in his arms, stroking her hair as his mind played through their imminent goodbye's.

"I won't say goodbye to you Cora. I can't. If I did, I would never leave." Knowing instead, he would hold her tight, look deeply into her eyes and tell her how much he loved her.

The time had come, the sun had risen. Leaning down to place a soft, lingering kiss on her luscious lips and then kiss her tears away, he squeezed her in his arms one last time. Dressed in his warrior tunic and armour, he picked up his belongings. With the weight of the World on his shoulders, he looked at her one last time through glassy eyes and told her, "I love you."

Watching him leave, Cora fell to the floor and sobbed with his words held in her heart. Crying about everything that had happened over the last months. Leaving her sisters, the Temple and being apart from the man she loved most in the whole World. Unsure of how she would ever get through the next month alone, she let her tears spill out on the floor.

There was no one there for her, not even to place an arm of comfort around her. For the first time in her life, Cora was truly alone.

Chapter 13

The first few weeks managed to drift by as Cora spent her time nurturing her plants, trying out new recipe's, along with her daily pleasure practices. Even making friends with her neighbours who didn't ask too many questions about her leaving the Temple. Often they would spend time in her courtyard together, cooking meals and discussing plants. Their young son enthralled with learning how to make vases out of clay. More often than not, making ugly clumps with holes dug out the middle.

It was the nights that Cora found the hardest. Wondering if Alexeii was all right or if he was lying harmed in a field somewhere. Thinking about what Helia was doing, knowing as the moon was dark, they would be preparing for their new moon ceremonies. She missed her Priestess life more so during the full and new moon's. A time where she would release what no longer served or be planting the seeds that would later come into bloom for her life with her Sisters.

By the third week, something in her broke. Believing that she would never be able to spend the next months alone every day, Cora prayed for the way to become clear to her that wouldn't leave her feeling so lonely. Eventually, 'the way' arrived.

The night before Alexeii's return, Cora's thoughts shifted from pure excitement to excruciating fear that he would never return to her. Desperate to see him again, yet knowing that she couldn't go through this again, not in this way.

Dreams about talking with her Goddess Persephone had brought ideas on what she could do, although she didn't think it had ever been done before. What she had was hope; if the Goddess had gifted her with this vision, she knew it was to make it happen in her life.

Knowing she wouldn't sleep, she went to her potter's wheel. Feeling the cold, wet clay beneath her fingers, allowing its shape to reveal itself. Often spending time creating Goddess statues to place in her garden. In honour of Persephone and to help her plants flourish. Each one with its distinct curves created by adding gentle pressure.

Losing herself in her craft, it wasn't long before the sun began to rise, the day had finally come when she would see her love again, she hoped. Laying her newly created statue out to start the drying process in the sun before being taken into the village to use the potter's kiln, Cora went to bathe and dress for Alexeii. Having created a rich oil from the lavender growing in her garden, she wanted to smell succulently sweet for him.

Not long after she had got ready and had finished kneading the bread to have with the goat's cheese and dates she had purchased the day before in the village, she heard their front door open. *He was here!* Running to greet him, she was taken aback by the wounded man who stood in her doorway. Limping towards her, a tired smile on his face, he dropped his helmet and bags and embraced her with one arm, his other bandaged up to his chest.

"My darling Cora, how I have longed for this day." Hearing the exhaustion in his voice Cora led him to their bedroom.

"How badly are you hurt? Sit here. I will get some ointments and clean bandages." Moving towards the door, Alexeii called her back to him.

"Stay with me for now Cora. Let me see your beautiful face. I didn't want to return to you in this way, but I couldn't be without you for another moment." Cupping her face in his hand, he looked at her intently. Falling into her big, blue eyes, he allowed himself to truly relax, the first time he had since he had left her a month before.

Spending the next few hours seeing to his wounds, cleaning, putting healing poultices on the worst ones and bandaging up the rest, Cora was horrified that some had already begun to get infected. The deep slashes from blades ripping apart his upper arm and lower leg. Not wanting to ask what had happened, Cora lay beside him, gently stroking his forehead.

It wasn't long before he was in a deep sleep. Knowing that he wouldn't have had any rest the whole time he was away, Cora left him sleeping to recover. Silently watching him, continuing to stroke his face, noticing the deep worry lines begin to release - content with just having him here, with her.

Leaving him to get the food and warmed mead ready for when he awoke, Cora busied herself while worrying about the conversation she knew she needed to have with him. It would be difficult for them both, not knowing how to approach it when he was so injured, unsure how long they actually had together.

Writhing about on the bed, calling out her name, Cora knew that he was having a nightmare. Coaxing him out of it with gentle whispers of incantations of peace and harmony, she saw him relax and his eyes flicker open.

"You are here! I dreamt that I had returned here and you were gone Cora." Fear gripped him so intensely that his worry lines had re-appeared. Reaching for her, moving his good arm around her to be sure she was actually with him.

Realising it was now dark, Alexeii asked how long he had been asleep, annoyed with himself for losing precious time with her. "Don't worry, you needed it. How are you feeling now? Are you hungry?"

"Ravenous." He replied, a twinkle of lust in his eyes.

"Not for that, my injured warrior!" She laughed, helping him to get out of their bed and leading him to the courtyard.

"It is gorgeous out here Cora." Looking around him, taking in the scented plants and lit candles, she undoubtedly had made this place a beautiful home.

Together they ate, Alexeii sharing some of the trauma's he had faced, Cora knew he was holding back from telling her everything, but she let him share what he needed to without pressing him.

"How long before you need to return?" Dreading the answer but needing to know so she could plan their time together.

Alexeii's eyes fell to the floor, unable to look at her as he shared the news, "Only two days. This war is messy; my men need me there; usually, I would have stayed with them, but I could not be without you one moment more Cora." Looking at her now, she noticed a tear fall from his face. Recognising his pain, she reached forward and wiped it away.

"I knew we wouldn't have long. I am just so grateful you are here and you are alive Alexeii." Kneeling beside him, she placed her head in his lap, feeling his warm hand stroke her, hot tears began to flow.

That night they made soft, sweet love to each other - both crying as they reached their peak of pleasure. Even with his wounds, he couldn't wait to be with her again. He had visualised their first night together, their hot passion, their need for one another. But this had been more beautiful than he could ever have imagined.

Having her in his arms, open to him, tender kisses placed around his wounds. His arousal massaged with warm, luscious healing oils, pleasure and love in potent alchemy of oneness. Feeling her rounded breasts brush up against his back as she stroked his shoulders, the delight of her legs wrapped around his waist.

Not being able to wait, he spun her around him with his good arm, laying soft kisses on her mouth, neck, breasts. Feeling her climb upon his erection, move on top of him in a smooth rhythm. Deepening into her, no, his imagination was never as good as the reality of being with his Goddess, his personal Priestess.

When he awoke the following day, he was surprised to see that Cora wasn't lying beside him. Getting up, he found her at her spinning wheel. Softly singing her incantations to herself, he stood and watched her in the early morning light, Cora unaware of his gaze.

Her thoughts of sharing the clear guidance she received from Persephone in her dream time kept her distracted. Hearing him clear his throat, she looked up. No longer the exhausted, injured warrior from the day before. Her Alexeii had returned; although still bandaged, he had lost that forlorn look. Standing in front of her now was her powerful, loving man.

Heart pounding, she got up from her spinning wheel, passion rising, she placed long lingering kisses upon his mouth. Still naked, she could see his phallus harden, wanting her.

"Not just now my love, first we eat." Laughing, she spun past him to get the bread from the night before, which she would dip in wine and feed to him, hoping that would then lead to sharing hers and the Goddess' future plans.

Laughing as she licked off the droplets of wine that fell to his stubbly chin, his tongue finding hers, locked in sensual kisses. Hands wandering over wanton bodies, unravelling the robes that covered her breasts, Alexeii removed his own cloths, which loosely covered his lower half. Lying on soft furs, he explored her body. Dipping fingers into goblets of wine and tracing them from her mouth down her throat, leaving a glistening trail between her breasts.

Moving lower to the opening between her thighs. Her juices rich and flowing. Sweet wine alchemising with her pleasure, he brought his fingers to his own mouth and tasted the nectar of wine and woman.

Alighting a spark of devilish joy in her, Cora followed the trail from his mouth, down his chest with her tongue, never taking eyes off his. Lower she travelled until she reached the hardness of his manhood.

Swirling her tongue, slowly over the head of his erection. Sensing his sharp intake of breath as pleasure sparked in his own body. Taking him fully into her mouth, feeling him shudder, the tenderness of tongue touching his sex, mouth encasing him. Eyes locked with eyes. The intensity of lust and love taking them to new heights.

Before he was ready to release, she climbed upon him. His hands guiding her hips as she rocked back and forth, taking her pleasure, giving as she received.

Watching her move on top of him was enthralling. Seeing the ecstasy upon her face as her desires spilt over her body - ample breasts with tight nipples calling to be held. Placing one hand over her breast, fingers softly circling her peaks. Moving his other hand towards her sex, fingers finding the tiny bulge of her clitoris, lightly stroking, releasing pulses of electric joy through her body.

His want now to taste her grew. He laid her down on the furs and moved down her body. His intention clear. Feeling his warm breath on her sex drove her wild. His tongue curling over her clitoris, sending shock waves through her. His fingers exploring her entrance as his mouth gently sucked, back arched Cora let out a moan of pure desire. Fingers and tongue dancing over and in her sex. She was so close to ecstasy, ready to melt at his touch.

Moving back up her body, kissing her deeply, he entered her. No longer able to wait to become one with her once more. Their unity was electric!

Witnessing her surrender to her ecstasy was intoxicating. Feeling his own sexual intensity rise, moving to the peak of his release. Both riding the waves of arousal, bodies glowing, moans of pure satisfaction filling the room. Serpents entwined in dance.

The build of passion was reaching its crescendo within her. No longer able to hold on, she let go, beautifully, without restraint. Pure sexual energy rippling through her. Her sex tightening around him with every wave of climax, the intensity releasing his own hot flow.

As he lay beside her, catching his breath, Cora let her orgasm flow over her, being in the moment of the Divine. Allowing herself to be held by his beautiful body. Arms around her, holding her to him. Their breathing beginning to slow. Unity, love and passion were theirs.

As the sensual after moments of lovemaking moved over them, Cora knew this was the moment to share her decision to return to the Temple. Morning conversations with the Goddess helped her to understand the direction her life must now take, even if it was a path not walked on before.

"Alexeii, I have something I need to share with you." Propping himself up on his elbow to see her face, he knew instinctively that this was important.

"I have struggled immensely this last month. Being away from you..."

"I know my love. I am so sorry. I really can't see another way." laying a soft kiss on her lips - the guilt of leaving her grabbing at his heart.

"Not only that. I miss my Temple, I miss being a Priestess..." Her words shocked him. Fear now locking round where guilt once held him. *Was she going to leave? Return to the Temple?*

Sensing his fear, Cora continued, "I don't want to leave you; in fact, I won't be leaving you Alexeii. That isn't even an option for me. I need you to know that." Relief unfurling the tension lines on his face with her words that she wouldn't be going.

"The guidance from the Goddess is that I will return to the Temple when you are in battle. I know you often need to be away for six months at a time. The strain on you to return to me sooner, I can see, is causing you stress." Eyes flickering momentarily away from hers, how intuitive this woman was, how well she could read him.

"It doesn't matter Cora. I would travel oceans to be with you for just one day. I don't want you to worry about me."

"But I do. I worry about our way of life, our soul purpose and how we can make it work for both of us. It is what I pray to the Goddess every day. She heard me Alexeii. She has shared her Divine plan with me."

"What is it she wants you to do?" Alexeii still confused with what Cora was proposing.

"Like Persephone, living six months in her village and Temple with her Mother and the other Priestesses and six months as Sovereign Queen of the Underworld with her lover and husband; I am going to propose to the High Priestess I do the same. Six months of the year I spend with you, during your time away from war. When you return to battle, for six months, I will return to my Priestess life."

"Will that be allowed? To be honest Cora, I'm not sure I could spend six months without you." Trying to work out how this would work, Alexeii had a million questions.

"I have no idea what the High Priestess will say. However, I do know that this is my path. The Goddess has given me instruction to make my plea to her. I know that six months would be hard. More than hard, it will be excruciating. Knowing that we will be reunited again, our love isn't forbidden. I believe it can be done. Our lives, our souls, require things of us, as well as our union. Do you see that?"

"I can. I don't like it, yet I can see how this can work. Unity of our past lives with our present to ensure a fulfilled future."

"Yes! Trust me when I say you will still be connected with me. The Goddess has shown me how. How I can communicate with you at a distance, through our Divine connection. Surely you have felt me as if I was there with you physically during our time apart."

Eyes widening at the realisation that he had felt her. Dreams so real that he could smell her sweet scent as he awoke. Times in battle where he experienced her soothing hands over him, healing his wounds. "That was you? You were doing that?"

"Yes my love, Persephone taught me Her ways. Your imagination isn't that good!" She joked with him.

"Ahh, so what now?"

"Today I need to return to the Temple and ask permission to return for six months." Feeling his arms tighten around him at the thought of her returning, not seeing her again for months on end.

"You leave tomorrow. Let me go today and speak with the High Priestess. I will return this evening and let you know what she says. If she agrees, which I have no idea if she will or not, I will enter back into the Temple for six months after our last day together." Eyes prickling with tears at the thought of being apart, yet Cora knew in her heart and soul this was right for them both.

"I love you Alexeii. I know you need to give your full attention to your men and the war you are fighting to keep us safe. Trust me, this is a blessing from the Goddess. A way in which we can live our lives together without losing who we are at our core."

"You believe the Goddess, your Persephone, will help create and support this way?"

"I know she will. Her guidance was clear."

Feeling contented that their future was now Divinely guided allowed Alexeii to breathe a sigh of relief. He knew that falling deeply in love with a Priestess meant his life would never follow a traditional path, surrendering to the wisdom she shared. His passion for her could overcome any challenge. For that, he was sure.

"When will you leave for the temple?"

"Not for a while..."

"Good." Pulling her close to him, they lost themselves in each other once more...

Chapter 14

Passing him the clay statue of her, which fitted perfectly in the curves of his hand, Cora shared, "This is a totem to take with you. To know I am always by your side, close to your heart."

Her return the night before was later than he had expected. Standing at the door, eyes red-rimmed, he knew that her time back at the Temple had been a challenging one. Fearing the worst, he wrapped her in his arms.

"It will all be well Cora, we will find another way."

"She agreed Alexeii. I am to return for six months."

"Truly? I presumed the reason you were so upset was that she had declined your request."

"No. It wasn't easy. At first, Ophelia was outraged that I would suggest such a thing, but after sharing the messages from Persephone and how she lived her own life, she couldn't really say no. I also saw Helia."

Bursting into tears at the memory of seeing her best friend after leaving without a goodbye. The hurt in Helia's eyes, Cora could still feel the rage boil over from her Sister when they finally met.

* * *

"How can you possibly ask me that Cora?"

"It was shown to me High Priestess, this is guidance from Persephone, I asked for the ways and she showed it to me."

Cora hadn't expected Ophelia to be so outraged. Believing it would be a cut and dry, yes or no, she didn't think her High Priestess would be angry at her even proposing the idea.

"For hundreds of years we have had our sacred ways. Lived the way we live and now, because you have found love outwith our walls, you want us to change the way we do things? Change our traditions?" Triggered by the audacity of Cora's request, Ophelia seethed.

If it were that simple would Ophelia herself not have had her own love by her side? Instead of years of pain and suffering.

"I understand that and no, it is not just for me that we should change our sacred ways. It is for the sake of the Temple, our future. I do not know why Persephone initiated me in this new transition that affects us all, but she has and for that, I am truly honoured."

Hoping that Ophelia would start to understand that this was indeed part of the inititation that had begun all those months before. The need to change things within the Temple walls, to transcend into a new way of being that was actually more aligned with Persephone and her teachings.

"I was prepared to never return here, even though it ripped at my heart, but something kept niggling at my surrender. I went to the Goddess with it and this was her solution. This is what she wants High Priestess. She knows what it feels like to be torn between loves. She herself torn between the love of her Mother and the love of her lover. It nearly destroyed her, destroyed them all! She learnt this way and it worked for her, so why would we not incorporate that within Her Temple?"

She could feel the anger that surrounded Ophelia start to dissipate. Her barriers to the idea beginning to soften as she recognised how much this was connected to Persphone's own story.

"I hear you Cora. What you are asking has never been done before. In all honesty, it saddens and, I must admit, angers me that this way was not gifted to me all those years before. That I had to choose and that always left a part of me broken."

Cora's heart went out to Ophelia. She knew the pain of having to choose and the loss when you did. Understanding why Ophelia felt so torn in accepting this new way.

"I know what you went through High Priestess; I know the pain. I would love it to be that no other Priestess or woman has to go through that again. I don't have all the answers, the path ahead is foggy but I know She has shown us this initial step so we can move in a direction that serves not only our soul's but our hearts too."

Tears streamed down Ophelia's face. She knew that to be true, that this way was a new beginning that felt more aligned with their Goddess teachings. To know that other Priestesses didn't have to experience the pain of having to pick between their soul purpose and their love, suddenly made complete sense.

"I agree Cora, I will grant this for you. We will find our way through it together."

Both Sisters embraced, knowing they had turned a corner in their relationship. Moving beyond the vibration of teacher and student and embracing the essence of equals, here to lead the way – together.

Ophelia asked Cora to find Helia, to tell her the news and hopefully build the bridges to their relationship. Dread filled her but knowing she had to reconcile with Helia before she returned, was something she needed to do.

Helia's rage had spilt over, projecting all her pain onto Cora. Accusing her of being selfish, a traitor, betraying their Priestess ways. Cora taking it all, realising the pain she had caused her beloved Sister. She didn't try to explain while Helia was in full flow of her anger. Instead, listening, hearing and honouring what she had done to hurt her.

Eventually sharing that she was genuinely sorry. Taking full responsibility for the pain she had caused. Caught off guard, expecting a fight, Helia's anger subsided. Making way for tears...

Helia looked at Cora. Sensing she had changed - seeing a strong, vibrant woman before her, realising that her own anger now felt juvenile. Perhaps not all to do with the loss of her friend?

"Why have you returned Cora?"

"I have been guided by Persephone, Helia. She gave me instruction to return for six months of the year, to Priestess duties, of worship to Her and to my work in the Temple." Searching Helia's eyes to see if she understood or if she would have to go through the whole ordeal again, as she had with Ophelia. Trying to explain, show her this was Divine guidance.

"I can see how that would work. I know you love him Cora; otherwise, you would never have left." The relief of hearing her Sister truly understand, not challenge nor question her, made Cora's heart swell.

"Thank you. Thank you for understanding. I do. I love him greatly. I love you too Helia. I have missed you so much." With wet faces, they embraced one another - a broken friendship on its way to reconciliation. It had been a long time since they had been together in this way. It felt like the missing piece in Cora's life had been found.

* * *

Cora's life would never be the same again. Finally, she felt fulfilled. Her life within the Temple was as Sacred as it ever was, perhaps even more so because she knew her time there was limited. Her days now filled with being of service to the Goddess instead of distractions until her love arrived home.

When Alexeii came back from war, they spent every moment together. Such delicious experiences of discovery and adventure. Sharing stories of the past six months with one another. Alexeii feeling more at ease that she wasn't alone when he was away. She was with her Sister's and her Goddess. It made their union all the more precious.

* * *

Looking upon her Priestess, Persephone's heart glowed. She knew the pain of being dragged away from all you have ever known for love. The hurt and loss often went hand in hand with love and pleasure. Believing in the process of alchemy, she knew that a life lived Divinely - knew both.

Her purpose was to gift Divine lessons and blessings to the life of The Passion Priestess and that is what she continued to do...

The End

ABOUT THE AUTHOR
Stephanie C Starla

Stephanie C Starla is a writer, poet, burlesque instructor, passion priestess and sexual energy coach from Scotland. This is her first piece of fictional work.

If you would like to follow her work and courses go to:

www.stephaniestarla.com
www.facebook.com/StephanieStarlaAuthor
www.instagram.com/stephaniecstarla/

Printed in Great Britain
by Amazon